"I could kiss you!"

Taryn's eyes lit up like a child seeing gaily wrapped gifts under the tree for the first time on Christmas morning.

Aiden's hands stilled peeling shrimp as he met her eyes. "I wouldn't mind if you do."

She sobered quickly at his invitation. "No, Aiden," she whispered. "We're not going to do that when your kids can see us." His blue-green orbs bored into her like heated lasers.

"I would never disrespect you by letting my kids see us in a compromising situation that would send them mixed messages. When I kissed you, it was something I'd wanted to do for a while. You're beautiful, intelligent and, even though you try to downplay it, you're sexy as hell. And I know if circumstances were different between us I'd definitely court you."

Her expression didn't change, although her heart was pumping as fast as a hummingbird's wings. Aiden had just verbalized what his eyes had been saying all along. He wanted her, but what they both wanted was impossible.

* * *

WICKHAM FALLS WEDDINGS:
Small-town heroes, bighearted love!

Dear Reader,

Welcome back to Wickham Falls, where you will meet a colorful cast of characters who run the Wolf Den, the legendary family-owned sports bar.

Single father, former navy SEAL and past military contractor Aiden Gibson is looking for someone to care for his daughters while he works rotating shifts at the Den.

Elementary schoolteacher Taryn Robinson is at a crossroads in her life. So when her old college roommate mentions Aiden needs someone to homeschool his preschool daughters, she jumps at the opportunity to leave the bright lights of the Big Apple for the small, rustic town in West Virginia's coal country.

Aiden is pleasantly surprised when Taryn applies for the live-in position. Not only is she more than qualified to homeschool his girls, but she's also incredibly beautiful. Taryn's presence makes him aware that his house is now a home and his daughters are thriving. While he finds himself attracted to the woman living under his roof, he is very careful not to cross the line to jeopardize his position as her employer.

Then sexual tensions simmering below the surface boil over until Taryn and Aiden are able to act out their fantasies. But when Taryn witnesses the darker side of the former military warrior's personality, she has doubts whether she will renew their contract for another year.

If you're looking for a dedicated teacher, a protective father and a family that will have you laughing, then I urge you to read *Her Wickham Falls SEAL*.

Happy reading!

Rochelle Alers

Her Wickham Falls SEAL

Rochelle Alers

HARLEQUIN® SPECIAL EDITION

Recycling programs
for this product may
not exist in your area.

ISBN-13: 978-1-335-46575-7

Her Wickham Falls SEAL

Copyright © 2018 by Rochelle Alers

Printed in U.S.A.

www.Harlequin.com

Since 1988, national bestselling author **Rochelle Alers** has written more than eighty books and short stories. She has earned numerous honors, including the Zora Neale Hurston Literary Award, the Vivian Stephens Award for Excellence in Romance Writing and a Career Achievement Award from *RT Book Reviews*. She is a member of Zeta Phi Beta Sorority, Inc., Iota Theta Zeta Chapter. A full-time writer, she lives in a charming hamlet on Long Island. Rochelle can be contacted through her website, www.rochellealers.org.

Her Wickham Falls SEAL is dedicated to
David and Juliet Johnson
and their precious adopted daughter, Chloe.

Behold, thou art fair, my love; behold thou art fair;
thou hast doves' eyes.

— *The Song of Solomon* 1:15

Chapter One

Taryn Robinson checked her reflection in the full-length mirror attached to the closet door. She'd selected a black wool gabardine pantsuit, white silk blouse and black suede booties to meet her prospective employer, who had informed her that she had passed his background check.

It had been ages since she'd had to interview for a job; the last time was years ago when she'd walked into a school building in downtown Brooklyn. At that time, she was a twenty-two-year-old with an undergraduate degree in early elementary education, a graduate degree in reading and a teacher certification. She had sought a position in a school where she could not only teach but also make a difference.

Her idealism had come from her social worker mother, who went above and beyond for her disadvantaged clients, and it was no different for Taryn, because she saw firsthand how some children had fallen through the cracks when she was a student-teacher in a less than desirable Washington, DC, neighborhood. However, she was realistic enough to know she couldn't change the world but only begin with one child at a time. Fast-forward nearly ten years, and she'd just resigned her position at that same school to leave all that was familiar to put down roots in a new state.

This was her third trip to Wickham Falls, the town with a population boasting less than forty-eight hundred residents and two traffic lights. The first time she'd come was to visit her former Howard University roommate, earlier that summer, and the second was to stand in as Jessica Calhoun's maid of honor when she married Sawyer Middleton.

Now she had returned to the house to dog-sit for the newlyweds honeymooning in the Caribbean, and interview for the position as a live-in teacher to homeschool single father Aiden Gibson's preschool daughters. Her backup plan, if Aiden decided not to hire her, was to apply for a position as a reading specialist or a permanent substitute teacher with the Johnson County school district where Jessica taught fifth grade. Taryn still could not believe that she was willing to trade the nonstop energy of New York City for the slow and easygoing pace of a small town in West Virginia.

It had taken a while for her to weigh her options on whether or not to relocate because she was at a crossroads in her life. She was thirty-two years old, soon to be a thirty-three-year-old, elementary schoolteacher living with her parents and grandmother, and the ninety-minute commute each way between Long Island and downtown Brooklyn had become emotionally and physically exhausting. There had been a time when her total daily commute was less than twenty minutes, but that all changed after she sold her condo to move in with her then boyfriend, who'd subsequently slept with her coworker *and* best friend.

Her mother had been devastated when Taryn revealed her boyfriend's betrayal, while her brother went ballistic, threatening to inflict bodily harm on the man who'd cheated on his sister. Taryn had to talk both off the proverbial ledge when she made arrangements for James not to be in the apartment when she went there to pack up her clothes and personal items.

She also wanted a clean break from the school in which she taught because every day she had to be around the colleague who'd deceived her. And instead of confronting the scheming woman, she ignored her as if nothing had occurred. There was no way she was going to lower her standards and fight with a woman over a man. Her mantra was "Men are like trains. There is always one leaving the station." It had been almost eighteen months since her last relationship ended and she was in no hurry to begin another one.

Although she would miss her parents, grandmother, brother, his wife and their children, she would not miss the traffic jams that added to her commuting woes. Sitting in her car for an interminable length of time on the Long Island Expressway, dubbed the world's longest parking lot, would become a thing of the past.

She'd spoken to Aiden the day before and he'd given her the directions to get to his house. Taryn wasn't certain why he wanted to homeschool his four- and five-year-old daughters, but she would find out soon enough.

She checked her hair and makeup for the last time, and then turned on her heel. Jessica's black-and-white bichon frise–poodle mix sniffed her shoes. "I can't play with you now, Bootsy, but Auntie Taryn promises to take you on a long walk around the neighborhood when I come back." Aiden had set up the interview for eight that morning because he was scheduled to be at his restaurant at nine.

Walking Bootsy had become therapeutic for Taryn because it gave her time to question whether she had made the right decision to give up all she had in New York to come to a place she never knew existed before Jessica moved there. Her initial reaction to Wickham Falls was that it was too quiet, too small and much too remote. There were no malls, fast-food restaurants, big-box stores or drugstore chains, and railroad tracks ran through the center of town. Moving to what locals called "The Falls" was akin to culture shock for Taryn, but she was willing to risk it because she needed to start over.

Taryn gathered her tote with the large envelope filled with the documents she promised to give to Aiden, left the house, locked the door behind her and got into her recently purchased late-model black Nissan Pathfinder. She'd put so many miles on her old car driving between Suffolk County in Long Island and Brooklyn that she feared breaking down when she least expected. She started the engine, programmed Aiden's address into the GPS and backed out of the driveway and onto Porterfield Lane. Lights, wreathes and Christmas decorations adorned many of the homes along the street. Most were tastefully decorated, unlike a few of the homes in her Long Island neighborhood where homeowners competed to outdo one another with lights, music and inflatables.

It took less than four minutes for her to arrive at the address Aiden had given her. She parked in front of a large three-story white farmhouse with a wrap-around porch, black shutters and matching front door. American and US Navy flags were suspended from porch columns. Taryn smiled. Aiden and her brother had something in common. Lieutenant Langdon Robinson was currently active navy.

She alighted from the SUV at the same time that the front door opened and a tall blond man sporting a military haircut walked onto the porch and waved to her. Now she had a face to go with the deep drawling voice with a distinctive Southern cadence.

Aiden's expression did not reveal his surprise when he approached the woman with whom he'd had several conversations about possibly homeschooling his daughters. His eyes met Taryn's large, slightly slanting light-brown eyes flecked with gold as she gave him a direct stare. If her intent was to make a good first impression, then she had made her point. Everything about her demeanor radiated confidence. And she was beautiful. Aiden found himself mesmerized by her round face and delicate features in a toffee-brown complexion.

He extended his right hand. "Aiden Gibson."

Taryn stared at his hand for several seconds before she took it. "Taryn Robinson."

He had lost count of the number of people he had interviewed to work for his family-owned sports bar, but suddenly Aiden felt like a gauche teenage boy meeting the girl on whom he had a crush. But then he had to remind himself that Taryn wasn't looking for a position as a server, busser, dishwasher or cook. She had come to interview for a position where she would share a house with him and his daughters.

Aiden released her hand. "Please come inside where it's warm." He led her up to the porch and into the house. "Have you had breakfast?" He knew he'd surprised Taryn when she gave him a questioning look.

"No. Why?"

"I thought we'd talk over breakfast. I know I asked you to meet me at eight because I was scheduled to be at the restaurant at nine, but my brother just called and offered to take the lunch shift at the Wolf Den. That's the name of our family's restaurant."

"Who watches your daughters when you're working?"

"It's been a merry-go-round with my mother, my sister, Esther, and occasionally my sister-in-law. My mother came up from Florida to stay with me for almost six months but went back because my stepfather was complaining that he missed her. Right now my sister babysits them whenever I work the night shift."

Taryn followed Aiden through the parlor, living and dining rooms with furnishings she thought of as classic farmhouse with oak-topped bleached pine tables. Area rugs with geometric designs covered polished plank floors. Off-white sofas and plush loveseats and chairs covered in prints and plaids in varying hues of pink and red flowers immediately caught her practiced eye. She had minored in art in college, and Taryn was always conscious of colors and symmetry.

"How often do you work nights?"

"I'm two weeks on and two weeks off." Aiden

wanted to tell Taryn it wasn't easy being a single father, yet he was willing to make sacrifices to afford his girls a stable environment. He pointed to the trio of stools at the breakfast bar. "Please sit down and relax."

Taryn sat and placed the tote on the floor. The kitchen was a chef's dream with stainless-steel appliances, white bleached pine cabinets, a built-in refrigerator/freezer, eye-level oven, microwave, twin dishwashers, a breakfast bar and nook with bench seats, and an industrial stovetop and grill.

"Are your daughters here now?"

Aiden shook his head. "No. They're in Orlando with their grandparents." He washed his hands in the smaller of two stainless-steel sinks and then slipped on a pair of disposable gloves. "What would you like for breakfast?"

"Oh, I get to choose?"

"Of course," he countered, smiling.

Lately, there hadn't been much for Aiden to smile about because it was as if his life was in limbo. The restaurant was down one cook and he'd had to put in more hours, which took time away from Allison and Livia. He also felt guilty that his mother, who should've been enjoying her retirement, was looking after his children. However, he never regretted divorcing his wife and being awarded full custody of their daughters.

Taryn rested an elbow on the granite countertop and cupped her chin on her fist. "Do you have a menu?"

His smile grew wider. *So*, he thought, *the pretty teacher definitely has jokes*. "Not available, but I'm certain I can whip up whatever you want."

A pair of light brown eyes met and fused with his bluish-green pair. "If that's the case, then I'd like a bagel with lox."

"Sorry, but I happen to be out of bagels."

Taryn scrunched up her pert nose. "Then I'd like a Southern breakfast: grits, fluffy scrambled eggs, crispy bacon, buttered toast and coffee."

I like her! Aiden mused, as he turned on the eye-level oven. It appeared she had a sense of humor, something that had been lacking with his ex-wife. Denise had claimed she had nothing to laugh or smile about because the townsfolks hated her and her family.

"That's one order I can fill. Do you want cheese in your grits?"

"Yes, please."

Aiden walked over to the built-in refrigerator/freezer to select the items he needed to prepare breakfast. Of all of the rooms in the house, he felt most comfortable in the kitchen. He'd grown up watching his father cook for his family, and once he entered adolescence he had been invited to join his father and uncles in the Wolf Den's kitchen.

"Do you cook?" he asked Taryn as he returned to the cooking island with eggs, bacon, a loaf of bread and a plastic bag of shredded cheddar cheese. Aiden placed strips of slab bacon on a baking sheet and sprinkled them with a shaker filled with brown sugar before setting the pan on a shelf in the oven.

"I do. But I prefer baking."

"That's where we differ. I love to cook, but I don't bake."

Taryn slipped off the stool, took off her suit jacket and draped it over the back of her stool. "Do you work weekends?"

"Right now I do, because we're down one cook. I'd like for you to clear up one thing for me."

"What's that?" Taryn asked.

"Why do you want to homeschool my daughters?"

Taryn leaned forward. "Why do you need someone to homeschool your daughters?"

Aiden went completely still and gave her a direct stare. "I asked you first."

"I can't answer your question until you answer mine. After all, Aiden, you're the one who put out the word that you were looking for someone to provide instruction to your children." They engaged in what Taryn thought of as a stare-down until Aiden nodded.

"You're right. I don't know if Sawyer told you about how folks in The Falls view my ex-wife's family."

"He's never said anything to me," Taryn admitted truthfully. She knew Jessica's husband had grown up in Wickham Falls.

"The Wilkinsons are considered the town's black sheep, and because my daughters share that bloodline they are looked down upon. Many of the parents in this neighborhood won't allow their children to play with Livia and Allison because they claim they're bad seeds. Rather than confront some of these narrow-minded adults, I prefer to have my daughters home-schooled until they're ready for middle school. By that time, they'll need to socialize with other kids their age and hopefully will be confident enough to hold their own against some of the bullies."

Taryn stared at Aiden as if he'd taken leave of his senses. She did not want to believe feuds like the Hatfields and McCoys were still happening. "Have the parents openly bullied your daughters?"

"Not to my knowledge. It's their kids who repeat what they hear their parents say."

"So they don't have any friends at all?"

"They play with their cousins."

Taryn was still attempting to wrap her head around the fact that Aiden's daughters were pariahs because of their mother. "I believe you made the right decision to keep them home at this age. However, I'm going to socialize your daughters and teach them what they should know."

Aiden's features softened in a smile. "Now that we're on the same page, I'd like to know why you prefer home-schooling to teaching in a traditional classroom."

Taryn tucked her shoulder-length, chemically straightened hair behind her ears. "Although I like teaching in a traditional classroom setting, it was the commute that wore me down. I drove, on average, three and a half hours each day, five days a week and most times when I got home, all I wanted to do was grab something to eat and go straight to bed. The next day, I was on the road at dawn to make it to work before eight. I hardly ever hung out after work with coworkers or friends because I had a fifty-five mile drive back to Long Island."

"What about the weekends?"

Taryn wanted to tell Aiden that she'd had a very active social life when she lived in Brooklyn, even before she moved in with her ex. There was always somewhere to go, new restaurants to explore and Manhattan was only a subway stop away. "If I went anywhere, it was usually on Long Island, because I didn't want to drive or take the train into the city."

Aiden filled a pot with water and set it on the cook-top. "Are you saying you're through with the big city?"

"You can say that." Reaching down into the tote, she removed the envelope. "I'm giving you copies of my teacher certification, certification in CPR and first aid, and several letters of recommendations that I'd sent to you. I've already resigned from my former school, so if you choose not to hire me, then I plan to apply for several vacant positions at Jessica's school."

"Did I say I wouldn't hire you?" Aiden questioned.

"You haven't said you would," she countered.

Aiden flashed a sheepish grin. "I must admit, I would've hired you sight unseen after the background check, plus Jessica told me you're a dynamic teacher. And being one of Johnson County's more popular teachers, I have to believe her."

"You don't think she said that because we're home-girls?"

"No. I don't know Jessica like that. I met her for the first time this past summer when she came into the Wolf Den with Sawyer. That's when I asked if he knew anyone looking for a job as a live-in nanny."

Taryn recalled her conversation with Jessica during her first visit to West Virginia. "When Jessica first told me you wanted someone to homeschool your girls, I wasn't ready to move down here because, initially, I thought Wickham Falls was too quiet."

Opening the oven door to check on the bacon, Aiden asked, "What made you change your mind?"

"I was still on the fence until my second trip. I spent most of the time relaxing on Jessica's patio, clearing my head and weighing my options. That's when Jessica reminded me that if I was tired of commuting, then I could always get a teaching position here because there were a number of vacancies at her school district.

Then I thought about how much I enjoyed working for a couple with young kids when I was a student at Howard University. I babysat and tutored, and seeing them excel was very rewarding. That's when I asked her for the phone number to your restaurant."

"So it was commuting that made you give up the bright lights of the big city for a life in rural West Virginia."

Taryn wasn't about to tell Aiden about having to work alongside the woman who made her question true friendship. She was also embarrassed that as a thirty-two-year-old professional woman she still lived with her parents. After she'd sold her condo, she had invested the proceeds with the intent of using it as a down payment on a house if or when she and James decided to marry. And she was certain she and her boyfriend would've eventually exchanged vows if not for interference from a third party.

"It definitely tops the list as to why I want to relocate," she half lied after a pregnant pause. It didn't top the list but rated higher than some of the other reasons.

Aiden walked over to the opposite end of the countertop and opened a drawer. "And because I don't want you to apply for a position with the local school district, I'm officially hiring you to homeschool my daughters." He removed a large envelope and a pen, and he handed them to Taryn. "You'd mentioned you wanted a contract, so I had my attorney draw up one for you. We didn't discuss salary, but this is what I'm prepared to offer you. If you agree to the terms, I'd like you to sign all three copies. I'll countersign them and give them to the attorney for execution."

Taryn removed the contract from the envelope and

perused it. When she glanced up, she noticed a hint of a smile tilting the corners of Aiden's mouth. He wasn't what she thought of as handsome, but rather ruggedly attractive. His face claimed too many sharp angles, and the bump on the bridge of his nose indicated it may have been broken at one time. However, it was the color of his eyes, a rich blue-green that reminded her of the warm waters of the Caribbean Sea that she found hypnotic. It was as if fire burned behind the brilliant orbs.

"How did you know?" she asked, once she recovered her breath. Aiden was offering her the same salary she'd earned from the New York City Department of Education.

"The investigator who conducted your background check told me," Aiden admitted. "I was afraid if I offered you less, you wouldn't take the position."

When Aiden had informed her he was going to have someone conduct a background check on her, Taryn had given him the information he needed to complete the investigation. She wasn't concerned that anything negative would surface when it came to her profession, but she was less than confident as to her personal life. She still could not believe she'd been so trusting, so naive when there had been obvious signs that her love life was in trouble.

Once she discovered her boyfriend had cheated on her, Taryn had not explained to her colleagues why she moved back to her parents' home. Nonetheless, the truth was revealed when her best friend, Aisha, invited James to accompany her to their faculty Christmas party. There had been whispers and shocked looks all around once everyone realized Taryn and James were no longer a couple. Gossip reverberated throughout the school building for weeks, while those who were bold enough to approach her and ask what had happened were disappointed when Taryn rebuffed their queries.

"It appears as if your investigator was quite thorough." Her voice did not reveal the inner turmoil she always felt whenever she recalled the shame and embarrassment of coming face-to-face with her ex-boyfriend and her best friend and colleague in the private dining room at a restaurant overlooking the East River. It had taken Herculean strength not to retrieve her coat and leave. She managed to stay until the end and then got into her car and drove home. Within minutes of walking into her bedroom, she went online and searched for vacation websites. It hadn't mattered that it was two weeks before Christmas and many of the airline deals were blacked out. Throwing caution to the wind when it came to price, Taryn decided to rent a villa in Fiji where she spent six glorious days detoxing from bad karma. She returned to the States tanned, rested and ready to start over.

"That's because I have to be able to trust you to be around my children. The contract is for a year, beginning January 1 with an option to renew or opt out thirty days before December 31. You'll notice I've included a clause where I'm willing to pay for your medical insurance. Once you give me your tax information, I'll have my accountant add you to our payroll. All employees get paid on the fifteenth and the last day of each month."

Taryn glanced at the contract again. The language wasn't filled with the legalese she would usually have to ask her attorney father to interpret. She picked up the pen and scrawled her name where indicated on all three copies, dated it and then gave them to Aiden to countersign. "It appears very straightforward."

"That's because down here most of us are plain-spoken. After breakfast, I'll give you a tour of the house and show you where you'll have your private quarters."

"Will I have space to set up a classroom?"

"Yes. The enclosed back porch and sunroom should give you more than enough space for what you'll need. A cleaning service comes in every Friday morning, so I don't want you to do any housework. And you don't have to concern yourself with cooking, because I'll prepare meals in advance for breakfast, lunch and dinner."

"When are your daughters coming home?"

"January 25. Why?"

"I'm going to need to order furniture and school supplies before I begin instruction. Once I return to New York, I'll order what I need from a teacher store warehouse and have everything shipped down here."

"There's a warehouse in Beckley where you can get most of what you'll need."

"Do they have desks?" she asked.

"Yes," Aiden said, as he added grits to the pot of boiling water and stirred the grains with a wooden spoon. "I looked them up online when I first decided to home-school my girls."

"What if I buy the supplies I need in New York and have them shipped to Jessica's house, and then when I come back, you can take me to Beckley for the furniture."

Aiden smiled and a network of lines fanned out around his large luminous eyes. "That'll work. I'm off tomorrow and if you don't have anything planned, I can drive you up to Beckley so you can select the furniture."

Now that she'd signed the contract, Taryn was committed to Aiden's children for the next year. "Okay. We're on for tomorrow."

Aiden lowered the flame under the pot of grits. "When do you plan to go back to New York?"

"December 30. I have to pack up my clothes and personal items and go to the teachers store and get the supplies I need for the classroom. If I get everything done in a couple of weeks, then I'll call and let you know when to expect me." Once she tied up all of her loose ends in New York, she planned to meet with a few of her former colleagues for a farewell dinner at one of her favorite Brooklyn restaurants before returning to West Virginia.

"You don't want to use a store down here?"

Taryn shook her head. "I'd rather go to the one I know will have the supplies I want."

"I'll give you a check to cover whatever you need to buy."

Taryn shook her head again. "That's not necessary. It's the middle of the school year and some items may be on sale, and coupled with my teacher discount, I may not have to spend too much."

"Make certain you give me the receipts so I can reimburse you."

She wanted to tell Aiden she wasn't concerned about him reimbursing her. The fact that she would earn the same salary and live rent-free, while not having to gas up her SUV at least twice a week was like winning top prize in a contest. And having a classroom of two rather than twenty-two made her feel as if she had been redeemed. "Tell me about your daughters."

Chapter Two

Aiden picked up an egg and cracked it in a glass bowl. "What do you want to know about them?"

Taryn admired Aiden's skill when it came to cracking eggs with one hand. "You told me they're four and five, which makes them very close in age."

"They were born eleven months apart. Allie just turned five and Livia was four in February."

So, Daddy was really busy making babies, Taryn thought, as she bit back a smile. "I'm going to test them before I decide whether to offer them the same instruction."

"I'm no teacher, but I'm going to go on the record to say that four-year-old Livia is as bright as her older sister. She's also what I think of as a free spirit. Right now she's into fairies. Last year, it was frogs."

"I like her already," Taryn said. "I must admit I was

partial to fairies and unicorns when growing up. What can I expect from Allison?" she asked, watching as Aiden removed the bacon from the oven and placed the crisp strips on a plate lined with paper towels.

"Allie is a true Gibson because she loves to cook. She's too young to touch the stove, so I allow her to sit on the stool and watch me."

Taryn found her mind working overtime as Aiden talked about his daughters while he brewed a pot of coffee, whisked eggs and dropped slices of bread into the toaster. He informed her he had activated parental controls on the television, their tablets and on his desktop. There were strict rules for bedtime, but he still couldn't get them to pick up after themselves.

"I plan to give them what students in a traditional school will experience. There will be instruction, recess and designated field trips. And given their ages, I will also assign a brief nap time."

"That's good to hear, because my mother complains constantly that Allie and Livia refuse to take naps. Most times, they'll just lie in bed singing or talking to each other."

Taryn made a mental note to devise a plan to get the girls to settle down enough to sleep for at least an hour. She wanted to ask Aiden about his daughters' relationship with their mother. Although he had been granted full custody, did they get to visit with her? She'd had students who'd lost one or both parents to divorce, substance abuse, imprisonment, terminal illnesses or domestic violence. Aiden had alluded that his in-laws were not viewed in a good light in Wickham Falls, and she wondered what his ex-wife had done to set the towns-folks against his children.

The aroma of brewing coffee mingled with the distinctive smell of bacon wafted to her nostrils. "Can I help you with anything?" she asked Aiden after a comfortable silence.

"No, thanks. I have everything under control."

Taryn waited for the weekends so she could choose between eggs, bacon, pancakes, waffles, biscuits, sausage or ham, grits and several cups of coffee with gourmet breads. Once a month she treated her family to Sunday brunch, which included mimosas, Bellinis and steak-and-eggs benedict, chicken-and-waffles or Belgian waffles with fresh fruit.

Aiden set two plates with napkins, coffee mugs and place settings on the breakfast bar. Minutes later, he ladled fluffy scrambled eggs onto the serving platter with strips of bacon, triangles of golden buttered toast and then filled the mugs with steaming black coffee. The bowl of grits and serving pieces were placed next to the platter.

"Do you want cream and sugar for your coffee?" he asked Taryn.

"Yes, please." Taryn stared at the dishes Aiden had prepared quickly and with a minimum of effort. "It looks too good to eat."

Aiden set a container of cream and the sugar bowl on the countertop and then sat next to Taryn, their shoulders mere inches apart. "You can sit and admire the food, but don't blame me when I eat up everything before you."

Taryn picked up a serving spoon and scooped up a serving of grits. "I did not sit here just to watch you eat."

Aiden speared several strips of bacon with a pair of tongs. "I love breakfast."

She gave him a sidelong glance. "Then we have something in common, because it's my favorite meal of the day. Unfortunately, I don't get to have a full breakfast until the weekends."

"That will change once you move in. Most times, I use egg substitutes for omelets and frittatas because I don't give the girls whole eggs more than twice a week."

Taryn resisted the urge to moan when she swallowed a forkful of grits and eggs. "I'm looking forward to having you cook for me. The grits are delicious."

Aiden leaned closer, their shoulders touching. "Do you like shrimp and grits?"

"Does a cat flick its tail?"

Throwing back his head, Aiden laughed loudly. "Should I take that as an affirmative?"

"It is," she confirmed. "Whenever I go to Charleston, South Carolina, to visit a cousin, I order it for breakfast, lunch and dinner. If I had to request a last meal, then it would be shrimp and grits."

"I had it for the first time a few years back, and I've tried recipe after recipe until I finally decided to use tasso instead of cured ham to give the dish a smoky taste."

"What's tasso?" Taryn asked.

"It's heavily cured ham that's smoked with a tremendous amount of seasoning. The result is dry, very salty, peppery and smoky. I only use a little bit because it can easily overwhelm a dish."

"Do you smoke your own meats for the restaurant?"

Aiden nodded as he took a sip of coffee. "Yes. Tomorrow, after we come back from Beckley, I'll take you to the Wolf Den and introduce you to my uncle and brother."

Taryn concentrated on finishing the food on her plate and she thought about how her life was going to change within a matter of weeks. She would leave New York and go from teaching in a classroom filled with twenty-two third-graders to homeschooling a four- and five-year-old. Instead of getting into her car and driving fifty-five miles to a school building, she would get up and walk to her classroom.

And living under Aiden's roof was definitely going to be an adjustment for her. The last and only man she'd lived with was James Robinson. When first introduced to each other, they had felt their meeting was predestined, the reason being that they shared the same surname. When she moved in with James, it was as a girlfriend. And once she moved in with Aiden, it would be as his daughters' teacher.

"Leave everything," Aiden said, as he clapped a hand on Taryn's shoulder when she reached for the platter. "I'll clean up later. I want to show you where you'll set up your classroom." His hand went from her shoulder to her arm and assisted her off the stool. "Right now the girls use the space as their playhouse. If you want, I can store their toys, dolls, bikes and dollhouse in the shed."

Taryn didn't know what to expect but the area down the hallway off the kitchen was much larger than she had anticipated and comparable to the average Manhattan studio apartment. It was at least five-hundred square feet. She walked over to the floor-to-ceiling windows with built-in pale-gray woven blinds. They were raised, allowing her a glimpse of an expansive backyard beyond the patio and outdoor kitchen. It was the perfect place for recess, where the girls could run around.

"What do you think?"

She shivered slightly when Aiden's breath feathered over her ear. He hadn't made a sound when he came to stand next to her. Taryn had a mental picture where she would place desks, bookcases, worktables and set up art, science and music corners.

Taryn turned to face Aiden. "It's perfect. Do you know the exact dimensions for this room?"

He nodded. "It's four-hundred and seventy-five square feet. Why?"

"I don't know if you have a set budget for furnishing the classroom, but I want to order a rug that's no larger than eight by twelve for my reading and library corner. My students always enjoy sitting on the floor whenever we have read-aloud."

Aiden stared at the terracotta floor. He had debated whether to cover the floor with indoor/outdoor carpeting once the sunroom was installed, but then he'd dismissed the idea when the floor installer suggested the stone because it was maintenance-free.

"You can buy whatever you need. Come with me and I'll show you your bedroom."

The salary he'd earned when employed as a private military contractor allowed him to pay off his mortgage, upgrade and enlarge the house, and put money away for his daughters' college education. He didn't think of himself as wealthy, but financially comfortable.

"How many bedrooms are in this house?" Taryn asked.

"Five. And that's not counting the one in the attic that doubles as my home office. When I first bought this place, it was only twelve-hundred square feet. Before Livia was born, I had a construction crew expand it on both sides, add the sunroom, mother-in-law suite, raise the attic ceiling, finish the basement and install central air and heat. Allie and Livia play in the sunroom whenever it's too hot or cold to play outside."

"Did you live here during the renovations?"

"No. We stayed with my aunt and uncle. It was a little cramped but we pretended it was an extended sleepover."

"How many bathrooms do you have?"

Aiden paused, counting. "Five. A half-bath off the kitchen, one in the basement with a vanity and commode, a full-bath in your suite, a bathroom in the attic with a commode, vanity and shower stall, and the original full-bath on the second story."

Taryn gave him a sidelong glance. "Should I assume you spend most of your free time in the basement?"

He smiled. "How did you know?"

"If you finished your basement, then it's obvious it would double as a man cave."

"Dudes need a place to drink beer, watch sports and trash talk without being censored."

"You can do that at a sporting event."

"That's true in big cities like New York and Philadelphia. Remember, West Virginia doesn't have any professional teams."

"Don't you go to high school and college football games?"

"Not really," Aiden admitted. "I enlisted in the navy right out of high school."

"How long did you serve?"

"Fourteen years." He had taken an oath at eighteen to protect his country and he'd fulfilled that commitment as a navy SEAL. Being away for extended periods of time had placed a strain on his marriage and whenever he returned home it was to a house in crisis. Nothing he'd done for Denise was ever enough and after a while he stopped trying to please her. She had complained bitterly that the house was too small for four people, so to appease her he used the money he'd earned as a private military contractor to expand it.

After the entire house was renovated Denise wanted to leave Wickham Falls and that's when he put his foot down. There was no way he was going to pick up and move after giving her what she'd called her dream house. Once their arguments had escalated to screaming matches, Aiden knew their marriage was in serious trouble. He'd suggested counseling, but Denise refused to go with him.

Aiden stopped at the end of the hallway. "Here's your room, also known as the in-law suite."

Taryn entered the sun-filled bedroom suite and felt as if she had stepped back in time when she saw the honey-toned, queen-size, hand-painted sleigh bed with a white goose-down comforter, lacy, sheer dust ruffles and mounds of matching pillows. She opened the door to a massive armoire to find a large flat-screen television and audio components. Stacks of linens, comforters and quilts were stored in the drawers of a smaller ornately carved armoire. A double mahogany dresser with a gilt mirror contrasted to the other pale furnishings. Taryn thought of the space as a lady's bedchamber and sitting room, with a sofa set on a straw rug and covered with yellow polished cotton and two flanking armchairs with hunter-green suede seat cushions. The suite was a quiet retreat where she could relax, sleep or just escape from the world around her.

Framed photos of Audubon prints were set on the mahogany desk and bedside tables. She walked over to French doors, which led out to the porch. It was the perfect place for her to begin the day with a cup of coffee or end it while watching the sunset. Pale yellow silk drapes could be closed to provide privacy or left open to take in the view of the distant mountains.

"I hope it's to your liking."

Taryn turned to find Aiden in the doorway, arms crossed over his chest. "It's more than I could've imagined."

His pale eyebrows lifted slightly. "You like it?"

"I love it." Taryn didn't say she would love it even more once she added her personal touch. She walked across the room and opened a door to a closet with overhead shelves. It wasn't as large as the walk-in closet in her Long Island bedroom but it would be adequate if she donated clothes she hadn't worn in years instead of packing them up and bringing them to Wickham Falls.

She opened another door to find a bathroom reminiscent of those in spas. Taryn could imagine herself whiling away time in the black marble garden tub with a Jacuzzi. A dressing table and chair were tucked under an alcove, while a vanity, freestanding shower with a large showerhead, commode, bidet and mirrored walls made the bathroom appear larger than it actually was.

"The suite gets an A-plus," she told Aiden once she returned to the bedroom.

He inclined his head. "I'm glad you're pleased with it. Now, are you ready to see the rest of the house?"

"Yes."

"We'll take the back staircase."

There was something about Aiden's body language that also prompted her to recall Langdon's, who'd bragged that all special ops had a particular swagger identifying them as military elite. She did not want to ask Aiden about his past because she didn't want to open the door for him to ask about hers. Taryn wanted their relationship to remain strictly professional.

Her single focus was educating his daughters and nothing beyond that. She had no intention of becoming his friend or replacing his wife as a mother for his children. She'd given up her condo to move in with a man who'd deceived her, and now she was giving up her home on Long Island to move in with a man who would become her employer. And she had a hard-and-fast rule never to engage in an affair with a supervisor or co-worker. She had witnessed firsthand the fallout and embarrassment when a first-grade teacher had been dating the school psychologist, who hadn't disclosed he was married, and was confronted by the man's pregnant wife after she showed up unexpectedly at the school building to threaten her husband's lover.

She climbed another flight of stairs with Aiden until they came to the third-story landing and his home/office/bedroom. A king-size platform bed, bedside table and a brown leather loveseat were positioned under an eave, while a workstation with a desktop and printer was placed in front of a window overlooking the front of the house. An entertainment stand held a television and stacks of DVDs. Taryn walked over to the credenza to study several framed black-and-white photographs. The image of an elderly couple sitting on a bench holding hands captured her attention. There were other photos of the same couple with the tall thin man dressed in his Sunday finery, while the short dark-skinned woman by his side wore a Native American beaded dress and moccasins.

"The woman is my maternal grandmother," Aiden said as he moved closer to Taryn. "Grandma Esther belonged to North Carolina's Eastern Band of Cherokee Indians. My sister is named after her."

Taryn's eyes went from the photographs to Aiden's features, noticing he'd inherited his grandmother's high cheekbones. "Is she still alive?"

"No. She died eight years ago, exactly one month to the day my grandfather passed away. My mother claimed she died of a broken heart."

"How did your grandparents meet?"

"That's a long story. I'll tell you about Grandma Esther's people another time."

Taryn wondered if Aiden had told his daughters that their great-grandmother's tribe had occupied what is now Western North Carolina for countless centuries. "How much time do you spend up here?"

"A lot, but only when the girls are away. Whenever they're here I sleep in the bedroom across from theirs as a safety precaution."

She did not want to imagine the consequences of someone attempting to break into Aiden's house. Given his size and military training, there was no doubt he would prove a more than worthy opponent. "Do you have a lot of crime in The Falls?"

"We have burglaries and vandalism, but it's been years since there's been a murder. Most of the break-ins are from kids hooked on drugs and looking for something they can easily sell so they can get their next fix.

Back in my great-granddaddy's day it was the revenuers chasing moonshiners, and now it's the sheriff and his deputies going after those dealing drugs."

"How large is the police force?"

"We have a sheriff and three deputies now that they've hired Seth Collier. Seth grew up here and enlisted in the Marine Corps. The sheriff got the town council's approval to hire him."

"How many folks from here join the military?"

"It has to be at least forty to fifty percent. Now that most of the mines are closed, boys who graduate high school have to find employment elsewhere. The recruiters from all the branches come during career week and have a windfall when they're able to sign up kids who can't wait to get out of The Falls. Some join and become lifers, while others use the military as a path to complete their college education."

"Like Sawyer?"

Aiden nodded. "I was a few years ahead of Sawyer but he was one of the smartest kids to ever graduate from Johnson High. He made straight As and had a near perfect score on the SAT. Everyone was shocked when he enlisted in the army instead of going directly to college."

Taryn smiled. "It looks as if he didn't do too badly." Jessica's software engineer husband had become a multimillionaire before turning thirty.

"He's done very, very well for himself. We're just glad he decided to come back *and* give back when he donated the money to create a technology department for the school district."

"Do you like working at the Wolf Den?" she asked.

Aiden gave her a lengthy stare, then said, "Yes, because I like cooking."

"Did you go to culinary school?"

A hint of a smile parted his lips. "Why would I go to culinary school to learn to prepare fancy dishes for patrons who can't pronounce or know what foie gras is? A cook by another name is a chef in his own realm. The Wolf Den has been run by Gibsons since the 1920s, and we continue to stay in business because we've established a reputation for grilling the best steaks and smoked ribs in the county."

Taryn laughed. "Okay, Chef Gibson, let's continue with the house tour." Jessica told her that she and Sawyer visited the Wolf Den at least twice a month because the food was exceptional and that Wickham Falls had only two eating establishments—the Wolf Den and Ruthie's, a family-style buffet restaurant. Jessica had disclosed that the townsfolks repeatedly voted down the town council's proposal for a fast-food chain, fearful it would impact Ruthie's viability. The Wolf Den would remain unaffected because they served beer and alcohol.

They descended the staircase to the second floor where Allison and Livia had adjoining bedrooms. Aiden's bedroom was opposite theirs, and a guest bedroom was at the end of the hallway along with a full bathroom. The girls' bedrooms were quintessentially girlish with white canopy beds, matching dressers and chests. Window seats were covered with brightly colored cushions stamped with animated Disney characters. Photos and figurines of fairies were in evidence in Livia's bedroom. Her older sister's bedroom was less whimsical with framed photographs of birds and flowers. Viewing the rooms gave Taryn a glimpse into the personalities of the two girls who were close in age yet differed when it came to their interests.

"Now, the basement," Aiden said as they again took the back staircase.

"I noticed the girls don't have a television in their rooms," Taryn remarked.

"There was a time when they did, but I had to take it out because they would turn it on late at night when they should've been sleeping. They aren't allowed in the attic, which means they can't watch television there. Your suite is off-limits, so again they're denied. I have a television in the basement with parental controls, and they're only allowed two hours of television a day because I don't want them addicted like some kids."

"Did you get rid of their TV?"

"No. It's in the basement storeroom. Why?"

"I'm going to need it for the classroom. Even though I didn't do it with my kids in New York because I taught third-graders, I'd like to designate Friday afternoon for free time and show age-appropriate movies, along with popcorn. If Daddy isn't working, then he's welcome to join us."

A flash of humor crossed Aiden's features. "I'd like that as long as I don't have to sit on a little chair."

"What if I order a beanbag chair for you?"

"I'd prefer a recliner."

She rolled her eyes at him. "Recliners are not allowed in the classroom."

"What if I string up a hammock?"

"Keep pushing it, Aiden. If your old joints pop and crack when you sit down, then I won't invite you to join us."

"I'm not *that* old."

"You've got to be at least forty."

"So the pretty lady has age jokes," he countered. "I thought it was women who were touchy about revealing their age."

"Not me. I celebrate every birthday all month long, and sometimes even longer."

"That's because you were born in the shortest month of the year."

"Don't hate on February because it's a month we celebrate. Eat Ice Cream for Breakfast Day, Super Bowl Sunday, Valentine's Day, National Gumdrop Day, Cherry Pie Day, National Margarita Day and, of course, Lincoln's and Washington's birthdays, and so many others too numerous to name."

"How do you know all of this?"

"I put up calendars on my bulletin board with all of the bizarre and unique holidays for each month and I'll talk about it for five minutes."

"You talk to children about margaritas?"

"Not the cocktail but the plant. I show them pictures of the blue agave plant, tell them where it's cultivated, how tall it can grow and that the high production of sugars, mostly fructose, is in the core of the plant."

"So it becomes a mini science lesson."

"Everything that goes on in my classroom is tied to learning, Aiden. Academics are important but I believe in educating the whole child, and that means making them aware of their environment. When a child goes shopping with his or her mother or father and sees a bottle of agave on the shelf, he or she will know that it's a sweetener and not a cocktail."

"I'm sorry for prejudging you."

"There's no need to apologize. You have every right

to question me about what I intend to teach Allison and Livia. I may not have any children but I, too, would be concerned if my child's teacher talked about alcoholic beverages, and I would never expose your children to something I wouldn't want for my own."

"I know I'm a little overprotective when it comes to my girls—"

"You don't have to say it, Aiden," Taryn interrupted. She wanted to tell him that she'd had students whose parents were dealing with their own personal issues and were unable to protect their children. She forced a smile. "Now, are you going to let me see your man cave?"

Aiden returned her smile with a bright one of his own. "Of course."

"This is ni-ice," Taryn drawled, drawing the word out in two syllables when she stepped off the last stair, her shoes sinking into the plush pale-gray carpeting that matched the fabric walls. Aiden flipped a wall switch and high-hats bathed the space in soft light. The basement had been transformed into a media/game room with black leather reclining chairs, sofas and loveseats. A flat screen measuring at least seventy inches was mounted on a wall for viewing throughout the expansive space. There was a wet bar fronted with a quartet of stools, a glass-fronted credenza with highball and cocktail glasses and fully stocked with spirits, along with a portable refrigerator and wine cellar. The game area contained pool and air hockey tables and additional side tables with checkers and chess pieces stood ready for willing players.

"How often do you entertain down here?"

"It varies. I usually host Super Bowl Sunday and alternate with my sister for Thanksgiving. My brother and his wife always have Easter and Christmas at their home. What about your family, Taryn? How do you celebrate the holidays?"

Taryn rested a hip against the mahogany bar. "My father is a rabid football fan and his guilty pleasure is attending the Super Bowl."

Aiden lifted questioning eyebrows. "He goes every year?" She nodded. "What does he do?"

"He's a family court judge."

Aiden grimaced. "Been there, done that," he mumbled under his breath. "What about your mother?"

Taryn knew if he'd gained sole custody of his children, then he would've had to have gone through the family court system. "She's a social worker."

"Do you have any brothers or sisters?"

"I have a brother who's active navy."

Aiden's expression brightened as if someone had suddenly turned on a light. "Where is he stationed?"

"Base Little Creek."

Recognition stole its way over Aiden's rugged features as he stared at Taryn as if she had spoken a language he did not understand. "Your brother is a SEAL?"

"Yes."

"He's SEAL Team 8?"

A soft gasp escaped Taryn's parted lips. "You know?"

"Yes, because I was a member of SEAL Team 5 stationed in Coronado, California."

She pressed her fingertips to her mouth. "I knew it," she said between her fingers."

"Knew what, Taryn?"

"I knew you were special ops because your body language is the same as my brother's. Do folks around here know you were a SEAL?"

Aiden shook his head. "Only my family knew. It was something my ex complained about because whenever I was assigned a mission I couldn't tell her where I was going."

Taryn thought about her sister-in-law who didn't complain when Langdon received his orders; she knew when she married him that she wouldn't hear from him for weeks at a time. "Didn't she know this when you married her?"

"Yes."

"I don't understand—"

"There's nothing for you to understand," Aiden said, cutting her off. "The only thing I'm going to say, and after that the topic is moot, is the best thing to come from my marriage is my children."

Although Aiden hadn't raised his voice, Taryn felt as if he had. She clenched her teeth to keep from reminding him that he had been the one to mention his wife. And she resented that he'd spoken to her as if chastising his children. "I'm ready to leave now." And she was. She'd spent almost two hours with Aiden, longer than any normal interview, and suddenly she felt as if she'd worn out her welcome.

"Don't you want to see the rest of the basement?"

"I'll see it at another time. I need to get back to the house and walk Bootsy." Taryn hadn't lied because she'd promised the puppy that she would walk him. Turing on her heel, she headed for the staircase, Aiden following. It only took minutes for her to return to the kitchen and retrieve her jacket and tote. "What time are we meeting tomorrow to go to Beckley?"

"Does ten o'clock work for you?"

She looped the handles of the tote over her shoulder. "Yes, and thank you for breakfast."

Aiden inclined his head. "You're welcome. I'll walk you to your vehicle."

Taryn wanted to tell him she could find her car without his assistance but decided to be gracious. "Thank you." Aiden walked her to where she had parked the SUV.

"Drive safely," he said when she opened the driver's-side door.

"I will."

She shut the door, started up the SUV and maneuvered away from the curb. Taryn acknowledged that she'd closed the door on one phase of her life, and when she signed the contract, agreeing to homeschool two preschoolers, she had opened another. Interacting with Aiden had been comfortable and easygoing until he'd mentioned his wife. And it wasn't for the first time she wondered, what had the woman done to result in her losing her children? Were the townspeople right when they claimed her family was bad news? And why, Taryn mused, did Aiden marry her when he knew her family's history, whatever that was?

The questions tumbled over themselves in Taryn's head, until she was forced to mentally dismiss them when she reminded herself that although she would share a house with her students' father, their relationship would be strictly professional. He was her employer and she his employee. It was something she could not afford to forget.

Chapter Three

Taryn stood at the French doors in Jessica's kitchen enjoying her second cup of coffee while watching the snow covering the backyard. Last night's lightly falling frozen precipitation had intensified into a full-blown blizzard. Her cell phone rang and she walked over and picked it up off the countertop. Aiden's name and number appeared on the screen. She answered the call after the second ring.

"Good morning."

"Is it really?" Aiden asked, chuckling softly.

She smiled. "It is for polar bears. It looks as if we're going to have to cancel our trip to Beckley."

"That's why I'm calling. The mayor has declared a snow emergency, which means all non-essential vehicles aren't allowed on the road. This is my only day off until after the New Year, so we won't be able to order the furniture until you return."

"Don't sweat it, Aiden. I'll order whatever I need once I get to New York and have it shipped to you. Do you want me to ship it to your home or the Wolf Den?"

"Can you arrange for it to be delivered to the house after you come back? Because I don't want to become a target for porch pirates."

"That shouldn't be a problem." There had been an escalation of porch thefts all over the country, despite homeowners installing security cameras. "Have you thought of installing cameras around your property?" Sawyer had wired the house with a system where he could view the house and greenhouses from remote locations.

"Yes and no."

Taryn walked over to the eating nook and sat down. "Either it's yes or no."

"Yes because it would make the house more secure, and no because we have a neighborhood watch. Many of my neighbors are retired and they are always on the lookout for any suspicious activity."

There came a pregnant pause before Aiden spoken again.

"What's on your agenda for today?"

"I'm going to put up several loads of laundry, dust, and vacuum and watch mindless television." She and Jessica had gotten along well when they shared an off-campus apartment because both were neat freaks. "What are you going to do on your day off?"

"Wait for the snow to stop and then get out the snowblower and clear the driveway and sidewalks for my elderly neighbor."

"That's very nice of you."

"Who's going to shovel for you?" Aiden asked.

"Jessica and Sawyer have an agreement with a few of the teenage boys on Porterfield Lane to rake leaves and shovel snow."

"I remember when I used to shovel snow for money before I started working in the restaurant."

"Can you answer one question for me?"

"What's that?"

"Why is the restaurant called the Wolf Den?" Taryn asked, not wanting their conversation to end. She liked listening to the sound of his drawling voice that was a constant reminder that he'd grown up in the South.

Aiden's deep chuckle caressed her ear when he said, "A family named Wolfe, spelled with the *E*, owned most of the mines in The Falls and several towns to the south. My family worked in the mines for more generations than I can count. My great-grandfather decided he'd had enough after he was buried for hours during a caved in and asked his brothers to go in with him making moonshine. They pooled their savings, bought a patch of land and built the restaurant under the guise they were offering hearty inexpensive meals."

"Were they?" Taryn asked, totally intrigued by the story.

"Yes, but they were also selling hooch. They'd buy several hogs from a farmer, butcher them and cook every part of them from the rooter to the tooter, and serve them along with rice, greens and cornbread. They charged fifty cents a plate and a dollar for a half-gallon jug filled with moonshine. Of course, they had to stay one step ahead of the revenuers or end up in jail."

"How did they do that?"

"They had paid lookouts and occasionally bribed the revenuers. When you come to the restaurant, you'll see that it's located off the road and down in a valley. The still was concealed up in the mountains and hidden among a copse of trees. Most times, you'd walk by it and not know it was there."

"Shame on you, Aiden. Your folks were criminals."

"I'd like to think of my folks as entrepreneurs. It was all about supply and demand. Once Prohibition was repealed, they exhausted their stock of hooch and went totally legit to concentrate on offering some of the best restaurant food in Johnson County."

"When I come back, I'm definitely going to sample some of your celebrated dishes."

"I know you're leaving in a couple of days, so if I don't talk to you, I'd like to wish you a healthy and happy New Year."

"I wish you the same."

Taryn ended the call and drained the coffee cup. Sawyer and Jessica were scheduled to return to the States on the twenty-eighth after their seven-day Caribbean honeymoon, and Sawyer's gift to Taryn was to pay for a round-trip flight on a private jet for housesitting and for when she planned to come back to Wickham Falls. He'd left the return date open because she still hadn't determined when she would leave New York. She had selected the thirtieth to return to New York because she wanted to ring in the New Year with her parents and grandmother. She wasn't certain whether her brother would be stateside, but his wife and children had come up from Virginia to celebrate Christmas with the elder Robinsons.

"Hey, baby," she crooned when Bootsy ambled into the kitchen and stood on his hind legs for her to pick him up. Taryn scooped him into her arms. "Did you have a good nap?" After she'd let him out earlier that morning to do his business, he had raced back into the house and curled up on his bed in a corner of the kitchen. While most dogs loved romping in the snow, Bootsy was the exception.

Bootsy turned around on her lap and then flopped down to rest his muzzle on her denim-covered thigh. She ran her fingertips over his black-and-white curly hair, wondering if the dog still missed his pet parents. He'd moped around for two days until Taryn picked him up and held him for several hours. She knew Jessica was going to have a hissy fit because she was spoiling her puppy, but Taryn was ready to explain that Bootsy had been experiencing separation anxiety and she had to comfort him.

Her cell rang again, and this time Jessica's name appeared on the screen. "What's up, Mrs. Middleton?"

"That's what I should be asking you, Miss Robinson. I just got an alert on my phone about the winter storm dumping close to a foot of snow on the Appalachians. Are you safe?"

"Safe as a bug in a rug," she quipped. "I'm here with Mr. Bootsy and we're going to stay indoors until the roads are cleared."

"Don't you dare attempt to shovel, because we pay the kids at the end of the block to clear away the snow along the driveway and sidewalk."

"Girl, please. The only thing I do with snow is watch it melt."

Jessica laughed. "I hear you. Sawyer's travel agent is making arrangements for us to fly into Huntington Tri-State Airport in Kenova, because it's closer to The Falls, and with the weather, Yeager Airport may have delays."

"Do you want me to pick you up in Kenova?"

"No. The agent is also arranging ground transportation."

"You're lucky you married a rich man, otherwise, you'd be among the huddled masses waiting to take a commercial carrier."

"Remember, I fell in love with Sawyer even before I knew how much he's worth, and if it hadn't been for you knocking some sense into my hard head, I'd still be single."

Taryn smiled. "I had to talk tough because you deserve to be happy. And don't forget, I'm a romantic at heart."

"Does this mean you're going to be open to dating a man if he shows the slightest bit of interest in you?"

"We'll see," Taryn said noncommittedly. She wanted to remind her friend that she had relocated to teach and not to find a lover or husband.

"How's Bootsy?"

"Spoiled rotten."

"Have you been holding him?"

"I had to, Jessica, he was experiencing separation anxiety. He wouldn't eat and moped around as if he'd lost his best friend. Either I spoil him or you can take him to a pet psychiatrist for therapy."

"Why do you always have to be a drama queen, Taryn?"

"You know I always have to be a little extra because my students love it."

"You should go back to school and get a degree in theater. You'd be perfect for the stage."

Taryn smiled. "I'm going to enjoy putting on plays with Aiden's girls."

"He hired you?"

"Yes."

"I knew he would because I couldn't stop singing your praises."

Taryn wanted to ask Jessica if she thought she couldn't get the position without her input but held her tongue. "I probably won't get to meet his children until the end of January. By the way, where's Sawyer?"

"He's jogging on the beach. I'm going to let you go because it's time for my cooking lesson. I signed up for a course to learn how to cook Caribbean-style roast pork."

"Yum!"

"Give my baby a kiss and tell him his momma will be home soon."

Taryn ended the call, set the phone on the table and bent over to press a kiss on Bootsy's head. "Your momma said to give you a kiss." The dog looked up at her as if he understood what she was saying. "I'm going to hold you for a little while longer, then I have to put up several loads of laundry and begin packing, because I have to go back to New York. But I will be back, and this time to stay." Any prior apprehension she'd had about relocating had vanished, and she now looked forward to starting over with a new position in a new state.

Aiden felt as if the first time he'd stood on the porch waiting for Taryn to arrive was on rerun. It had been almost three weeks since she sat in the kitchen sharing breakfast with him. She had updated him as to what she had purchased for the classroom: the desks, chairs, bookcases, worktables, a supply closet, beanbag chairs, cots, white boards and bulletin boards; all of the items were scheduled to be delivered to his home the next day. The black Pathfinder came into view at the same time he came down off the porch.

He signaled for her to pull into the driveway next to his SUV. She cut off the engine and Aiden opened the driver's-side door. He held out his arms and wasn't disappointed when she rested her hands on his shoulders as he assisted her down.

"Welcome home."

Aiden couldn't pull his eyes away from her face as he drank in her natural beauty. He had welcomed her back because she would now share his home. He had told his daughters about Taryn, and once they returned to Wickham Falls, they should be prepared to begin school. Spending their days playing with each other and visiting their cousins would become a thing of the past. They had to begin their formal education before they fell too far behind their contemporaries.

Taryn lowered her eyes, smiling. "Thank you."

He peered inside the Pathfinder. Boxes filled every inch of the cargo area. "What on earth did you buy?"

She tapped a button on the remote and the hatch opened. "Not all of the boxes are filled with school supplies. Only the ones marked *CLASSROOM*."

Taryn had had her clothes, sewing machine and school supplies shipped to Jessica's house ahead of her return. Her leaving New York hadn't been without melodrama—especially from her mother. Mildred Robinson had questioned whether Taryn knew what she was doing, while suggesting her running away had to do with her being constantly reminded of James's duplicity whenever she encountered his current lover. Taryn had given up trying to convince her mother that she had gotten over James and let her go on and on as to how she allowed one man to turn her off of the opposite sex. And the night before her departure, her mom came into her bedroom and confessed that she hadn't wanted her to leave because since moving back home, she had gotten used to having her daughter around.

She had reminded her they would still live in the same time zone and if she decided to fly to Wickham Falls, it would take approximately three hours. Her explanation seemed to pacify her mother, even though it hadn't stopped the older woman from shedding tears when it came time for Taryn to leave; her mother hadn't been that emotional when she and her dad drove Taryn to college as an incoming freshman.

Taryn waited for Aiden to stack boxes and carry them inside the house before lifting a wheeled Pullman and carryon with her clothes and personal items and following him. Aiden had welcomed her home and she felt as if she *was* home. Her first order of business was putting her personal style on the bedroom suite before she unpacked the school supplies.

She had five days to organize the classroom before Allison and Livia arrived, and she'd decided to give them time to reconnect with their father before beginning instruction. Taryn returned to the vehicle to remove two quilted totes at the same time Aiden cradled a trio of boxes against his chest. "Show-off," she said, winking at him.

"If you'd eaten your spinach this morning, you'd be able lift more than five pounds."

She scrunched up her nose and pushed out her lips. "For your information, I had a spinach-and-feta omelet this morning." Once the jet reached cruising speed, the in-flight chef had prepared breakfast for the eight passengers. A car service awaited her when the plane touched down in Charleston at ten, and when she arrived in Wickham Falls, she found the Pathfinder loaded with everything she'd had shipped to the Middleton residence. The night before, Sawyer sent her a text indicating he'd loaded her vehicle, but wouldn't be there to meet her because he and Jessica would've left for school.

Aiden shifted the boxes. "Don't worry about coming out again. I'll bring in the rest."

Taryn wasn't going to argue with him; she was anxious to settle in and begin decorating the would-be classroom before the furniture arrived. When she'd left The Falls, the snow had begun melting when temperatures rose above freezing, which had now returned to an unseasonable sixty degrees. She had dressed in layers and she couldn't wait to shower and change into something cooler. Stripping off the sweatshirt and long-sleeve T-shirt, Taryn made quick work of emptying the luggage and hanging up jackets, coats, suits and dresses. Her summer clothes were in under-the-bed storage containers. She had also downsized her closet and donated clothes she hadn't worn in more than a year.

"Where do you want these?"

Taryn turned to find Aiden holding the storage containers. He looked at her as if she was an intruder and when she saw the direction of his eyes, she realized he was staring at her chest. The sheer plum-colored camisole with a built-in bra revealed a lot of flesh, but the strategically placed embroidered black lace flowers over her nipples provided a modicum of modesty. "Please leave them by the door."

* * *

Aiden swallowed to relieve the dryness in his throat. When he'd walked into Taryn's bedroom, he had not expected to see her wearing the revealing top. His body betrayed him, while reminding him of how long it had been since he'd slept with a woman. Placing the containers on the floor, he backed out of the suite, walked stiffly back to the kitchen, slumped down onto the bench seat at the breakfast nook and waited for his erection to go down.

He closed his eyes and exhaled a long audible breath. Aiden acknowledged that he found Taryn beautiful, but refused to acknowledge that he found himself attracted to her the way a man was attracted to a woman. And acting on his physical reaction to her would prove disastrous. His children would lose their teacher, and he could be faced with a lawsuit if Taryn decided to sue him for sexual harassment.

He'd successfully completed the rigorous SEAL training necessary to be awarded the trident pin, and now he felt as if he was being tested again, not physically or mentally, but emotionally. Aiden had sacrificed having a relationship with any women following his divorce for his children. He hadn't wanted to expose his daughters to women with whom they would bond and believe would possibly become their stepmother.

Waiting until he was back in control, Aiden returned to Taryn's vehicle to bring in the last box. He had lined fourteen cartons in varying sizes against the wall. All of them were labeled with their contents. Computer, printer, laminator and reams of paper were among the many items she had packed. Nothing was more important to Aiden than his children's education and he didn't want to do anything that would sabotage that goal, even if he found himself physically attracted to the woman who would be teaching them.

He walked out of the house and sat on an all-weather porch chair. Stretching out his long legs, he crossed his booted feet at the ankles. He had exchanged his day off with his uncle to be available for Taryn's return and switched to a night shift the following day, so he would be there for the scheduled morning furniture delivery.

Aiden looked forward to having the house filled once again with the sounds of his daughters' voices, even when they threw hissy fits if they didn't get their way. There were times when he'd find himself studying his children as if waiting for them to exhibit some of the more negative traits in their mother's personality. Denise had been sullen, argumentative and a complainer. Nothing he'd done made her happy or appreciative. Every time he returned from a mission, it was to a house in total turmoil. Allie and Livia cried and whined and fought with each other without the slightest provocation, and Denise was overwhelmed having to keep the house clean and take care of two toddlers.

He'd lost track of time when he registered a slight click and came to his feet as the storm door opened. Taryn had changed into a pair of black stretchy cropped pants, white cotton pullover and white ankle socks and running shoes.

"Do you mind if I join you?"

Aiden smiled. "Please do." He waited for Taryn to sit on the chair next to his before retaking his seat. The subtle scent of her perfume wafted in the air. She looked like a young college coed with her bare face and her hair styled in a ponytail.

She returned his smile. "Is it always this warm this time of year?"

"No. There are times when we experience June in January. Mother Nature is playing with us because some of the young trees are putting out buds."

Taryn rested her hands on the arms of the chair. "She can play a little bit longer because I'm enjoying the warmer temperatures." She closed her eyes. "I'm going to sit here a while before I start unpacking the boxes in the classroom."

"Why don't you relax and do it later. I'm not going to work today, so I'll help you."

"Do you have a ladder?"

"Yes."

"I'm going to need it to put up a banner."

"I'll put the banner up for you," Aiden volunteered. "I also need you to give me the receipts for your purchases, so I can write a check."

"No rush, Aiden. Have you told your children that they're getting a teacher?"

He nodded. "Yes. And they're really excited that they're finally going to school."

Taryn turned and met his eyes. "Did you tell them the school would be in their home?"

Aiden nodded again. "That's what got them excited. Allie said it will be fun to have their own classroom, while Livia asked if their cousins were coming to their school."

"What did you tell her?"

"I told her not now. I don't think she would've understood the reason why her cousins go to the public school, while she and her sister will remain here."

"How old are their cousins?"

"They range in age between four and seven. My brother has two boys and my sister two girls."

Taryn paused. "I plan to follow the district's elementary school calendar, so whenever classes are cancelled for school holidays or professional development, I don't have a problem with them coming over."

"Are you sure? I don't want you to become overwhelmed."

She gave him a you've-got-to-be-kidding-me look. "Looking after six kids is a cakewalk when compared to dealing with twenty-two. I'll plan outdoor activities that will include dodgeball and teaching them to jump double Dutch. Maybe, down the line, you can get a basketball hoop and volleyball net. And if we're forced to stay indoors, then it will be board games, movies with popcorn or baking cookies."

Aiden's eyes caught and held hers. "You're going to teach my nephews to jump rope?"

"Don't athletes, boxers in particular, jump rope?"

"Yes, but double Dutch, Taryn?"

She narrowed her eyes at him. "Do I detect a hint of sexism in your question?"

"No! How can I be sexist when I have two girls?"

"Men have mothers and sisters, yet that doesn't stop them from being misogynists."

"Please don't lump me into that category, because I like women."

Taryn smiled as if she'd won a small victory. "So you don't have a problem with me teaching your nephews to jump double Dutch?"

"No. But…" His words trailed off when Taryn leaned over and put her hand inches from his face.

"No buts, Aiden. Please let me handle this." She

wanted to tell him that boys from countries all over the world entered international jump rope competitions. "Most young kids spend too much time sitting and playing computer games when they should be playing outdoors. My parents grew up on New York City sidewalks jumping rope and playing stickball. During the summer months, they'd only come inside to eat and then go back outside." Taryn paused. "I believe in educating the whole child and that translates into mind and body. Phys ed will become an important component of your daughters' daily instruction, along with yoga and meditation."

"What's up with baking cookies?"

"It'll become a math lesson when they have to recognize numbers within a recipe. I hope you don't mind if I use your kitchen?"

"Why should I mind, Taryn? After all, you live here."

"I just don't want to be presumptuous."

Aiden studied her for a full minute. "You really have it all figured out, don't you?"

"After teaching for ten years, I hope I have it figured out." Taryn knew she should begin to tackle the school supplies, yet loathed getting up and going inside. "I really could spend the rest of the afternoon right here, but I have to unpack." She'd spoken her thoughts aloud.

"Don't stress yourself, Taryn. You have the rest of the day to unpack. And I told you I would help."

"Thank you." Aiden's volunteering to help was certain to make setting up easier. She closed her eyes and slumped lower in the chair.

"Whenever you're ready I'll take you to the Den for lunch."

Taryn opened her eyes. "Ready!"

Throwing back his head, Aiden laughed loudly. He pushed off the chair, stood and gently eased Taryn to her feet. "We'll leave as soon as I get my keys and lock up."

"I'm going to get a jacket."

Taryn wasn't willing to challenge Mother Nature. The temperatures may have echoed spring, but the calendar indicated it was still winter. She slipped on a lightweight quilted jacket, scooped a small shoulder bag off the sofa and retraced her steps. Aiden stood at the front door, arms crossed over his chest. She'd been truthful when she told him she was ready. Ready to settle down in a new state; ready to educate his children and ready to live with a man who had become her employer.

Chapter Four

"The Wolf Den looks like a hideaway." Taryn stared through the windshield at the building, which suddenly appeared out of nowhere in a forested area after Aiden turned off the local road and down an embankment.

Aiden pulled into a reserved parking space with a sign bearing his name. "When you're engaged in illegal activity, you try not to advertise it."

Taryn looked at the man who didn't seem remotely bothered that family members had straddled the line between legal and illegal activities. Her eyes lingered on his high cheekbones, square jaw, strong chin and firm mouth. Although she preferred to date men of color, there was something about Aiden she found very appealing, and she knew it was his dedication to raising his daughters as a single father. What she wanted to but could not ignore was the virility coming off him like waves of shimmering desert heat. She realized she hadn't been unaffected when he walked into her bedroom to find her in her camisole, and neither was he when she recognized the lust in his startled, hungry gaze. The single incident was enough to remind her to close the door unless fully dressed.

"Where was the still?"

"It was about a mile up and over the hill." Aiden placed a hand on her wrist when she released her seat belt. "Don't move. I'll help you down."

Taryn waited while Aiden got out and came around the Suburban. He opened the passenger-side door and extended his arms. Resting her hands on his shoulders, his fingers tightening on her waist, and with minimal effort, he swept her off the leather seat and set her feet on the ground. Reaching over her head, he closed the door.

She stared at the one-story clapboard building. A sign over the door with the image of a snarling wolf was the only reference that identified the business establishment with the parking area crowded with pickups; the mouthwatering aroma of grilling meat filled the air.

"Something smells wonderful."

Aiden took her hand. "There's a smoker out back along with a smokehouse. We've been smoking ribs, brisket and pork since the Den opened. Last year, my uncle decided to add the smokehouse and a smaller building so we can cure ham and age steaks."

"What do you recommend?"

He gave her fingers a gentle squeeze. "I know I sound a little biased, but everything we make is delicious."

Taryn lifted her eyebrows. "Only a little?" she asked.

Aiden held the door for her. "Wait and see for yourself."

Waiting until her eyes adjusted from coming out of the bright sunlight and into the restaurant's dim interior, Taryn got her first glimpse of Aiden's family-owned dining establishment. The Wolf Den was a sports bar, restaurant and beer garden. Gaslight wall sconces and matching pendants over the booths harkened back to a bygone era.

A chalkboard listed craft beers and another had the day's specials. There were a number of flat screens, muted and tuned to various sports channels; half a dozen booths lined one wall, and most of the tables and stools at the mahogany bar were occupied. Regulars greeted Aiden with nods or fist bumps, while waitstaff moved quietly and efficiently around the restaurant. Those exiting café doors carried trays filled with dishes from which wafted the most delectable aromas.

"I thought you were off today."

Aiden smiled at the waitress who'd come over to clean off an empty table. "I am. Taryn, this is my cousin, Sharleen Weaver. Sharleen, Taryn Robinson."

Taryn nodded to the middle-aged waitress with fire-engine red hair. "It's nice meeting you."

Sharleen's bright blue eyes sparkled. "It's nice meeting you, too, honey. Where has Aiden been hiding you?"

"She's Allie and Livia's teacher," Aiden said.

"That's wonderful news," Sharleen said. "It's about time those babies got some schooling."

Aiden pressed his mouth to Taryn's ear. "Let's go," he whispered, "before Sharleen talks your ear off."

Aiden held the café door as Taryn preceded him into a spacious kitchen. Two men working side by side were multitasking, grilling steaks, burgers and loading plates with French fries and onion rings. The older of the two, a white bandanna covering his head, glanced up and smiled at her.

"So you're the one my nephew has been bragging about." Wiping his right hand on the bibbed apron, he extended it to Taryn over the partition. "Jonah Gibson."

Taryn's smaller hand disappeared when his fingers closed over hers. "Taryn Robinson."

Jonah's green eyes sparkled like polished emeralds. "Welcome to the Den."

Aiden, resting his hand at the small of Taryn's back, nodded to the fry cook. "Taryn, the young man next to my uncle is my cousin Thomas Johnson. Tommy, Taryn."

Tommy flashed a shy smile. "Nice meeting you, ma'am."

Taryn returned his smile. "Same here." Aiden had introduced her to Tommy as his cousin despite the younger man claiming a complexion reminiscent of dark chocolate mousse. She wondered if they were actually related or had referred to each other as cousins like kids who have "play cousins." She had lost track of the number of students who'd regarded one another as cousins when in reality they shared no bloodline.

"How's it going, Tommy?" Aiden asked him.

Tommy wore a black sweatband under a white baseball cap. "It's all good."

"Keep up the good work."

Jonah pulled the clapper on an overhead bell and then set a plate with grilled steak, French fries and onion rings under warming lights. "Pick it up!" he shouted. "Sorry about that," he said, winking at Taryn. "What can I fix for you?" he asked her in a softer tone.

Going on tiptoe, Taryn peered over the partition. "I'll have the meat loaf with mashed potatoes and gravy and collard greens."

Aiden dropped his arm. "There's a table in the corner with a staff-only sign. Sit there and I'll bring you your plate."

Taryn walked through the out door at the same time that Sharleen entered the kitchen to pick up her order. She found the table with seating for four in a corner near an emergency exit door. When Aiden mentioned the Wolf Den was a family-owned restaurant, it was obvious it was also a family-run eating establishment.

Sharleen approached the table and set a mug of stout on a coaster. "That's for Aiden. What can I get you to drink, honey?"

"I'll have the same." It was the first thing that came to Taryn's mind. She was in a sports bar, so drinking beer was the norm. There had been a time when she and a small group of teachers gathered at their favorite pub for wings and beer. A smile parted her lips when she recalled the good times she'd shared with her colleagues. Although she would miss their camaraderie, she was also looking forward to reconnecting with the teachers who taught with Jessica and Sawyer.

One night a month, Jessica got together with three fellow teachers for a girls' night out. Kindergarten teacher Beatrice Moore left the group after her husband's company relocated to Denver, and Jessica and the other three women had invited Taryn to take Beatrice's place to complete the quartet. Jessica informed her that they alternated eating at her house, because she didn't have any children, or at a local restaurant before driving to the next town to bowl.

Getting together with Abigail Purvis, Carly Adams and Jessica would vary from her get-togethers with her former colleagues because all of the women were married. When Taryn thought about her own marital status, she had come to the realization that she did not need a man to make her feel fulfilled or to complete her. It had taken her thirty-two years to realize that she really liked Taryn Melissa Robinson; that she was secure enough to move to another state to live with a stranger and commit to educating his children.

Reaching across the table, she picked up the mug and took a sip. Her eyebrows lifted in surprise. She'd expected the brew to be bitter, but it had a dark, smooth, smoky complex of chocolate and coffee. Taryn had drunk more than half the beer when Aiden returned, balancing steaming plates.

Taryn stared at the dishes he set on the table. One had her meat loaf and sides. Another was brimming with a steak salad with romaine, crispy onions, tomatoes and crumbled blue cheese, while samples of pulled pork, barbecue ribs and burned ends were piled high on the third plate.

"Who else is eating with us?" she asked Aiden.

"It's just you and me." He winked at her. "I want to give you samples of customer favorites."

"The portions look like more than samples."

Aiden sat down next to Taryn. "Think of it as la-dinner."

"What on earth is la-dinner?"

"It's a combination of lunch and dinner, like breakfast and lunch is brunch."

Taryn tried not to laugh when she saw the devilish

look in Aiden's eyes. "Did you come up with that all by yourself?"

"Yes I did," he admitted proudly. "If you mention la-dinner to the girls, they'll start crying."

"Why?"

"One time I fed them a heavy meal around three in the afternoon and decided they didn't need to eat anything for the rest of the day. As I was putting them to bed, Allison asked if they were going to eat dinner. Once I explained they'd had la-dinner, they burst into tears, claiming they'd only eaten two meals when they were supposed to have three."

"Shame on you, Daddy. I should report you to the authorities for denying your babies food," Taryn said, teasingly.

Aiden tugged at her ponytail. "So it's going to be three against one."

Taryn smiled. "That's girl power." She picked up the mug and took a long swallow. "I really like your beer."

"My beer?"

"Yes. Sharleen left it for you, but I decided to take a sip."

"You did more than take a sip."

Taryn patted his shoulder. The sweater concealed muscles as hard as dried cement. "Sharleen's bringing another one, so you can have it."

"Thank you so very much," he drawled.

"Do you only hire family?" she asked in between forkfuls of tender, slightly spicy collard greens.

"Now we do. There had been a time when my father and uncle thought about closing down because they were losing so much money. The bartender didn't ring up half the drinks, while the waitstaff were pocketing tips instead of sharing them amongst themselves. Then it was the food stock. It was as if cases of steaks, racks of ribs and boxes of chickens had taken legs and walked out."

A slight frown appeared between Taryn's eyes. "Did they find out who was stealing?"

"Not really. Dad and Jonah couldn't work the kitchen and watch the front at the same time. So they fired everyone, shut the doors for a couple of months and when they reopened it had become a family-owned *and* family-run business.

"My mother and aunt volunteered to wait tables; my sister manned the cash register and my brother tended bar. Employing family did the trick. Once Sharleen's kids were out of the house, she came on board. She watches her grandchildren at night whenever her daughter works the night shift."

"Is it as busy for dinner as it for lunch?"

"It varies. We close on Sundays, which allows everyone a day of rest."

Taryn angled her head, giving Aiden a lingering stare. "How does Tommy fit into the family unit?"

"He's my mother's nephew. Her younger sister and brother-in-law met in the army. Tommy said he hated being a military brat; he graduated college with a liberal arts degree and couldn't decide what he wanted to do. So he called Jonah and asked to work for him, and the rest is history because we were short one cook."

"Your family is quite the racial mosaic."

"Does that bother you?"

"Of course not. Do you think I'm intolerant?" Taryn didn't want to believe she had given off vibes that she was judgmental when it came to race and sexual preference.

"I don't know what to believe because I don't know you that well."

"How true, Aiden. The only thing you know about me is on paper." A wry smile parted her lips. "After we live together for a while, you'll know enough not to judge me."

She picked up her fork, cut into the meat loaf and popped a piece into her mouth. The meat melted on her tongue. Taryn knew it was impolite but she couldn't stop making moaning sounds as she took another bite. "Who made the meat loaf?"

Aiden went completely still when he stared at Taryn. Eyes half closed and the moans escaping her parted lips reminded him of a woman in the throes of passion. It was the second time within hours that his children's teacher reminded him that he'd been denying himself female companionship. And the last thing he wanted was to fantasize about making love to her.

There were occasions when his mother would take her granddaughters to Florida for several weeks where he could have sought out a woman to sleep with, but something wouldn't allow him to engage in what he thought of as a one-night stand. Even in high school, when most of his classmates were sleeping with different girls, Aiden preferred having a steady girlfriend. Something in his brain would not let him sleep with more than one woman at a time.

"It's Jonah's recipe," he said after an interminable pause.

"This is the best meat loaf I've ever eaten. Are you going to let me in on the family secret?"

"My uncle grinds beef, veal, pork, turkey and duck and then adds the house seasoning. He lets the meat marinate overnight, tops it with seasoned breadcrumbs and barbecue sauce, and bakes it in a pan with a rack to catch the juices. Whenever someone orders meat loaf he puts a slice on the flattop to add a little crunch."

"It sounds laborious, but the result is worth it."

Sharleen came over and set a mug of ice-cold beer on the table in front of Taryn. "Enjoy." She spied the empty glass. "Aiden, do you want me to bring you another beer?"

"Nah. I'll just drink this one." He grasped the mug, put it to his mouth and took a deep swallow. "Don't forget to save room for the barbecue," Aiden said to Taryn after Sharleen walked away.

Taryn placed a bite-sized rib, several brisket burned ends and a forkful of pulled pork on her plate. "I cannot see myself eating like this every day."

"You could if you make it your biggest meal of the day."

"Yeah, right. And take a nap as soon as I push myself away from the table."

"That's when you go for a walk," Aiden suggested.

"Walking around here is certain to be a workout because of the hills."

"That's because we're in a mountainous region."

Taryn nodded. "I did get to see the waterfalls that gave the town its name. I admit, they are spectacular."

"I must have been crazy, but as a kid we'd challenge one another to climb to the top of the waterfalls and dive off into the rapids."

"You had to be crazy," she said. "You could've been killed if you'd hit your head on the rocks."

"That's what my mother said when I came home with cuts and bruises because I'd misjudged my dive. The coach of the high school's swim team suspended me for a month, and the result was we lost the state championship that year because my replacement couldn't match my speed. As the captain, my teammates blamed me for the loss, and they wouldn't have anything to do with me until the following school term when we had to try out again for a spot on the team."

A slight frown creased Taryn's forehead. "I don't understand. Why would you have to try out again when the coach knew what you could do?"

"He was sending a message that I had to be taken down a peg. Scouts from several colleges had come to the school to watch me swim, and a few were extending full athletic scholarships."

"Why didn't you accept them?"

"I would've considered it if I hadn't had an in-depth interview with a navy recruiter. When he told me what was required to become a SEAL, I was hooked. It didn't matter that I would be thrown into a pool with my arms tied behind my back or endure sleep deprivation during Hell Weeks with more than one hundred-thirty hours of drill. I'd become an adrenaline junkie looking for the next fix."

"My brother admitted he was ready to quit halfway through but managed to stick it out. He said earning that trident was his greatest achievement, second only to the birth of his children."

"He sounds like a man after my own heart," Aiden said, smiling.

Lines fanned out around his eyes that were the result of, despite wearing sunglasses, squinting in the desert sun. Aiden had never felt more alive than he did whenever he embarked on a mission with the members of his team. It was as if he'd flipped a switch in his brain and in that instant he'd become a naval commando.

Aiden knew his tenure as a SEAL was limited because as he aged he realized his body could not sustain the physical challenges the missions required. And once he married and became a father, Aiden started counting down the time when he would resign from the navy. However, his thirst for the next pursuit continued after he was recruited by a private military security company to work for them; they made him an offer he could not refuse. He'd been paid extremely well when he rescued the kidnapped daughter of a wealthy family in a country Americans were cautioned not to visit.

He continued to work for them, leaving home at a moment's notice until his late father's eldest brother passed away. Jonah asked for his help running the restaurant and that's when Aiden knew he had to step up and do what Gibson men had done for almost ninety years—keep the Wolf Den open.

"Does your brother intend to become a lifer?"

Taryn swallowed a mouthful of pulled pork. "He says he does. My sister-in-law told me Langdon would like to be assigned to a carrier or warship, but she's trying to convince him to get a desk position at the Pentagon because their kids don't see him enough."

"What about you, Taryn?" Aiden asked. "Would you ever consider becoming a military wife?"

"No, only because I see what my sister-in-law is

going through. I'm not going to marry a man to have a half-time husband and father."

He gave her a sidelong glance. "So you're not opposed to getting married?"

Taryn met his eyes. "No. It's just that I haven't met the right guy."

"What would constitute the right guy?" The seconds ticked by as they stared at each other.

"Someone I can trust."

"So trust is the most important component. What about love?"

She blinked slowly. "Without trust, there is no love."

"Is that what happened to you?" Aiden asked. "Your boyfriend cheated on you." His question was a statement.

"Yes," Taryn said before she could censor herself. "I could've dealt with his cheating, but it's not easy when he cheats with your colleague and supposed best friend."

"What a piece of garbage!" Aiden spat out.

"I agree."

Aiden moved his chair closer until their shoulders were touching. "Do you want to talk about it?"

"Not really. I've already said too much. I'm not comfortable talking to strangers about my private life."

"What you tell me will not go beyond this table. And now that we're living together, you have to stop thinking of us as strangers."

"Living with a man is what changed my life."

"How?"

Admitting she had lived with a man now opened the door on her past. *What do I have to lose?* she thought.

She had to trust Aiden not to repeat what she was going to disclose. "I met James at a health club where we were both members. We connected because we shared the same last name. After working out we'd go to a local coffee shop and talk for hours. After a couple of months we began dating and a year later James asked me to move in with him. It took a while before I agreed because it meant selling my condo."

"Did he ask you to sell your condo or did you volunteer to sell it?"

"It was my decision to sell rather than hold on to it."

"Why?"

"We'd begun talking about marriage, and it didn't pay for us both to own condos."

"Why didn't he move in with you?"

Taryn replayed Aiden's question in her head. It was same thing she'd asked herself over and over. "Instinct told me not to give up my place, but at that time I'd been so blindly in love with James that I thought I would lose him, but in the end I did anyway. When I confronted him after finding him in bed with my friend, he didn't bother to apologize. He told me I could either stay or leave. He said it was his apartment and because we weren't married, he did not have a problem with us seeing other people. I was very proud of myself when I didn't lose my temper. I calmly told him that I was leaving and that I would be back with my brother to get my things. I warned him not to be there when I came with Langdon or it wouldn't end well for him."

Aiden dropped an arm over her shoulder. "Did he heed your warning?"

"You bet he did. My brother is very intimidating. He's six foot six and weighs a solid two-sixty, and one punch from him would've broken James's jaw. I took what I needed and loaded up Langdon's SUV, left the keys on the coffee table and locked the door."

"What about your so-called best friend?"

"I saw her every day and treated her as if she did not exist." Taryn told Aiden that none of the teachers knew why she'd moved back home until the night of the faculty Christmas party. "Once Aisha showed up at the restaurant with James, some of the other teachers wanted to take her into the bathroom and confront her, but I told them she wasn't worth it. I made a vow that I will never allow a man to talk me into doing something I don't feel completely comfortable with again."

"Good for you. If the slug cheated on you with her, then she'll cheat on him with another man. And I don't blame your brother for wanting to jack his ass up. I would do the same if my brother-in-law got funky with my sister."

"Other than my immediate family and Jessica, you're one of the only people to know the whole sordid story about my past love life."

"What is important is that you got out unscathed," he whispered. "It wouldn't have been so easy if you'd been married or had children. It's the children who are always the losers in a divorce."

She turned her head, their mouths only inches apart. "Are you talking about Livia and Allison?"

Aiden pulled back, his eyes darkening with an unnamed emotion. "Yes. Thankfully, my girls weren't privy to what went on between me and their mother, but every once in a while Allie will bring up something, which leads me to believe that she remembers what her mother said or did to her."

"Some children can remember things as far back as three, while with others, it's five." Taryn smiled. "I'm really looking forward to meeting your daughters."

Aiden grunted softly under his breath. "The only thing I'm going to say about my children is that they're going to prove to be quite a challenge."

Taryn rolled her eyes upward. "Please don't talk about challenges. More than fifty percent of my students had problems some people don't experience until they're adults."

"It's no different here in The Falls, Taryn. Just because we're a small town doesn't mean that we only have small-town problems. I'm certain if you talk to Jessica, she'll tell you about some of her at-risk students."

"Speaking of Jessica, she invited me to join her and several other teachers for their monthly Friday girls' night out."

"Don't worry about it, babe. Go out and have fun I'll make arrangements for the girls to stay over with my sister the weeks I work nights."

Taryn's body stiffened in shock. Had the endearment slipped out because Aiden had a habit of calling women *babe*? Or perhaps she was reading more into his sweet talk than need be. She forced a smile. "Thank you."

All conversation ended when both concentrated on eating. Taryn was relieved that she'd told Aiden about her breakup with James. Now he knew her stance when it came to living with a man. It had been her decision to move to Wickham Falls to homeschool his children for the year, and if she decided not to continue, then she could opt out, apply for a position at the public school level and possibly put a down payment on a small house. In retrospect, Taryn realized James cheating on her was more of a positive than a negative. It had allowed her to examine her life and where she wanted to take her future, and right now her future was in Wickham Falls. It was as if the big city girl had found her rightful place in the world.

Chapter Five

"What do you think?" Taryn asked Aiden.

Aiden shook his head in amazement. The enclosed porch and sunroom had been transformed into a classroom. Areas were set up for science, art, music and relaxation. Beanbag chairs were positioned to have an uninterrupted view of the television. Taryn had ordered a low table and chairs where Allison and Livia would eat their lunch.

Oak bookcases were partially filled with DVDs, picture and chapter books, and a number of board games. All of the shelves and compartments in the oak supply closet were labeled: paper, art supplies, crayons, paints, pencils, markers, glue sticks, paper clips and rubber bands. Bulletin boards and colorful maps depicting the world, the United States and West Virginia were affixed to expandable cloth-covered panels, which created a faux wall without putting nails or screws into the existing walls.

The desks, including Taryn's, were set up with eastern exposure to take advantage of the early morning sunlight. His heart swelled with pride when he noticed Taryn had placed a laminated plaque bearing the name of each girl on their desks. A rug stamped with letters of the alphabet and corresponding pictures of animals and plants in the reading corner matched the room's banner. She had also purchased cots, which were stored in a corner next to the supply closet. A large canvas bin was filled with balls, jump ropes, a badminton net, rackets, shuttlecocks and volleyballs for outdoor play.

"They are going to be so excited when they see this."

"I'm excited just looking at it," Taryn admitted. "I have a few days before they arrive, so that gives me time to print out the calendars for bizarre and unique holidays and put up January's on the bulletin board." Turning, she smiled at Aiden. "I couldn't have gotten it together so quickly if you hadn't helped." The truck with the furniture had arrived at eleven that morning, and four hours later, the classroom was complete.

"You saved a lot of time when you unpacked the supplies yesterday." Aiden glanced at his watch. "I have to go and relieve Jonah. Are you sure you're going to be okay staying here by yourself until I come back?"

"Stop stressing, Aiden. And I promise not to throw a beer pong party while you're gone."

Throwing back his head, he laughed, the sound reverberating throughout the space. "What do you know about beer pong parties?"

"Enough," she said. "All frat boys need are red cups,

ping-pong balls and cheap beer, and the craziness is on and popping."

Aiden sobered. "I think I'm going to take your suggestion and install a security system. I don't like the idea of you being here alone with Allie and Livia whenever I work nights."

Taryn wasn't going to try and talk Aiden out of securing the property. In the past, he'd left his daughters at his sister's house overnight. But now that they were entering school, Taryn had volunteered to look after them whenever their father worked the night shift.

"I'm going to be all right," she said as he continued to stare at her. "Remember, I house sat for Jessica and Sawyer when they were on their honeymoon. Now please go before you get fired."

Dressed entirely in black, Aiden appeared larger, and radiated a virility that drew her to him like a magnet. It had taken only days for Taryn to realize it wasn't going to be easy living under the same roof with Aiden because he was a very attractive man, with an easygoing manner that made her feel comfortable whenever they were together.

He gave her a snappy salute. "Aye, aye, boss."

Taryn followed Aiden to the front door and quickly locked it to keep out the cold air. The weather had changed overnight, the temperature dipping to midtwenties. Tonight would be the first time she would be alone in the house until Aiden returned sometime after midnight. Turning on her heel, she walked to her bedroom. She had eight hours until Aiden's return to do whatever she wanted, and taking a long leisurely bath was the first order.

* * *

Aiden unlocked the Den's side door and came face-to-face with his uncle. "How was business today?" It was something he asked whenever he prepared to take over cooking for the nighttime customers.

Jonah, removing the bandanna from his shaved pate, flopped down on a bench. "It's slow as frozen molasses."

Aiden patted Jonah's shoulder. His uncle had recently celebrated the big 6-0, and had more energy than men half his age. Tall and powerfully built, Jonah was no-nonsense when it came to running the restaurant, but over the years Aiden had come to the conclusion that Jonah was a big dog with a big bark and no bite.

"If it doesn't pick up, then I'll close early." Aiden took off his street clothes and changed into chef's pants with a houndstooth pattern and a black tunic. He exchanged his work boots for a pair of running shoes.

"What do you think about us closing at two once lunch ends, and reopen again at five for dinner?"

"I like that idea," Aiden admitted. Peak hours for serving lunch were between eleven and two, and five and ten for dinner. "When do you want the change of hours to go into effect?"

"The second Monday in February. That should give everyone almost three weeks to get used to the change."

Aiden wondered if it was enough time to alert their regulars. "I'll send out an email to those on our mailing list. I'll also have to call *The Sentinel* and alert the editor to change our hours of operation in our ad." They'd placed an advertisement for the restaurant in the local biweekly for years to in order to support the newspaper, which had been steadily losing advertising revenue needed to sustain its viability.

Jonah clapped a hand over his mouth and closed his eyes. "I guess that's a go," he said, then opened his eyes. "By the way, how's your teacher doing?" he asked.

Sitting down on the bench, Aiden tied the laces on his running shoes. "She finished setting up the classroom. One of these days you have to come over and see it."

Stretching his legs out in front of him, Jonah sandwiched his large hands between his knees. "She sure is a beauty."

"Oh, you noticed."

"Hell yeah, I noticed. I'm sure you did, too."

Aiden met his uncle's eyes. Jonah and his wife had been married for nearly forty years and never had any children. They'd unofficially adopted their niece and nephews, and Aiden remembered spending as much time at Jonah and his Aunt Becky's house as he had his own. Now it was Jonah and Becky's turn to open their home to Tommy.

"I did." Did Jonah expect him to lie?

"Does she have a special fella?"

Suddenly Aiden's face went grim. "What's up with the interrogation?"

Kicking off his shoes, Jonah reached down to massage his sock-covered feet. "There's no need to get your nose out of joint, Aiden. I just asked you a question about Taryn. Either she does or she doesn't."

"She doesn't. Why?"

"A couple of guys were asking about her."

"They can keep asking, and you can tell them from me that she's not interested."

"Have you become her mouthpiece, son?"

"No, Uncle. It's just that she had a bad breakup with her last boyfriend, and from what she's told me, I don't think she's ready to get involved with anyone right about now."

"What about you, Aiden?" Jonah asked.

"What about me?"

"Don't you think it's time for you to start dating again? After all, it's been almost two years since you broke up with Denise."

Aiden reached for a baseball cap and covered his hair. "I didn't break up with her. She was the one that didn't want to be married or a mother. I gave her an out when I initiated the divorce and took Allie and Livia. And when am I going to have time to date with my work schedule and taking care of the girls when they're not in school?"

Jonah stood. "I can change your schedule so you can have weekends off."

"We'll talk about this later. I need to get in the kitchen and help Tommy." He picked up a bibbed apron off the stack on a shelf and slipped it over his head. "Tell Aunt Becky that I'm going to bring the girls over to see her once they get back."

"She'd like that. Right now she's in heaven, babying Tommy. I keep telling her he's a grown-ass man and doesn't need another mother, but she won't listen. I think that's the reason he spends so much time here, so he won't hurt her feelings."

"You should know after all these years that Aunt Becky is the quintessential nurturer. Now stop massaging those big dogs you call feet and go home and kiss your wife."

"Yeah, yeah, yeah," Jonah mumbled under his breath.

"Love you, Uncle."

Jonah smiled. "Same here."

Aiden walked into the kitchen to find Tommy cleaning off the griddle. "How was business?"

Tommy's head popped up. "Not good. I don't know what's up, but I don't think we had more than three customers since lunch. Let's hope we get a decent dinner crowd."

"Jonah and I talked about shutting down after lunch and reopening for dinner. That should give us time to prep for the next day's specials instead of waiting until closing time."

"That sounds good to me."

He studied his younger cousin. Thomas Johnson had inherited his father's tawny-brown complexion and his mother's straight black hair and delicate features. He'd noticed an increase in the number of young women who'd frequented the Den since Tommy's arrival. It was apparent that they were quite taken with the tall, slender man, whose shy smile matched his quiet demeanor.

Hiring Tommy was a natural fit for the Wolf Den. He'd worked as a part-time short-order cook while attending classes at the University of Michigan.

Aiden glanced at the chalkboard listing the day's specials: beef and barley soup; chicken-fried steak; Texas short ribs; and red beans and sausage.

"What are the day's desserts?" he asked Tommy.

"Red velvet cake and sweet potato pie."

Sitting on a stool at the prep table, Aiden picked up the notebook where Jonah jotted down suggestions for the next day's special. His uncle had listed southern fried chicken, chili con carne and lentil soup.

"I'm going to start on tomorrow's specials. Do you think you can handle the walk-ins before we start dinner?"

"No problem," Tommy said confidently.

Aiden retrieved a crate of whole chickens from the walk-in refrigerator/freezer. He dumped the chicken in an industrial sink filled with cold water. Meanwhile, he filled a large plastic bin with buttermilk and added the house seasoning. Once he washed and cut up the chicken, the pieces would soak in the buttermilk and house seasoning overnight. Working quickly, Aiden emptied a sack of dried red beans into a stockpot to soak and reduce the cooking time.

Time passed quickly when he went out back to the smokehouse and selected links of smoked sausage for the lentil soup. Aiden decided to make the soup and once cooled, refrigerate it because the flavors in lentils, like split peas, improved over time.

Sharleen entered the kitchen and attached her order to the ledge above the stovetop. "We have a couple of latecomers."

Aiden peered at the shorthand notes on the slip. "Two chicken fried steaks with white gravy, mashed potatoes and sweet-and-sour cabbage."

Sharleen applauded. "You're the only one who can read my chicken scratch. Most times, I have to translate for Jonah and Tommy."

"Maybe if you wrote a little more legibly, they'd be able to read what you've written."

"I took a speed writing course years ago, and I find it helpful when I have to take an order."

"Well, now that Aiden has translated, I'll take care of this order," Tommy volunteered.

* * *

The bell over the door chimed at 5:30 p.m., and Aiden left the kitchen to see who'd come in for dinner. Sharleen had gone home and her daughter wasn't scheduled to arrive until six. He recognized the three men. They were regulars who preferred sitting at the bar. He greeted each by name, filled three lager glasses with beer from the tap and returned to the kitchen. It was only after they drank their first glass that they would decide what they wanted to eat.

A steady stream of customers filled the Den for dinner and Aiden lost track of time as he and Tommy worked side by side, filling orders. Tommy's workday began at eleven and ended at eight. Once the last customer left, Aiden locked the front door, retreated to the kitchen and packed away leftovers, which would be picked up the next day by someone from the local church for their soup kitchen. The tradition had been established by Aiden's father two decades ago and was still in effect years after he'd passed away.

"I cleaned the tables and swept up."

Aiden's head popped up and he smiled at his brother-in-law. Fletcher Morgan had come onboard to tend bar at night the year before when his hours as a mechanic at a used car dealership were cutback. He and his sister, a dental hygienist, were saving to buy a larger house because with two children they wanted each girl to have her own room.

"Thanks for everything, Fletcher."

"Anytime, brother. I'll lock the door on the way out."

Aiden glanced at the wall clock and smothered a groan. He'd hoped to be home before midnight, but that wasn't going to happen tonight. He still had to unload the dishwasher, sweep and mop the kitchen, and put out the garbage for the morning pickup by the carting company.

There were times when Aiden wondered if his life would've been different if he'd accepted the athletic scholarship to join the swim team for a Florida college. His parents had given him their full support because they wanted him to earn a college degree, but the lure of enlisting in the navy, to be afforded the opportunity to see the world won out. The recruiter told him what he wanted to hear and in the end, he turned down the scholarship, much to his parents' disappointment—his mother, in particular. Braden and Ruby had wanted Aiden to become the first in their families to graduate college. Aiden managed to redeem himself with Ruby when he became a SEAL, an elite brotherhood of twenty-five hundred big and buff spies and commandos who conducted clandestine maneuvers for their government.

His team had been involved in various missions from rescuing a CIA analyst held hostage by a terrorist group in Somalia to extricating an undercover FBI agent whose cover was blown after he'd infiltrated a domestic sleeper cell, and others in which several of his team members had sustained wounds that had ended their careers. Aiden had been lucky because in the fourteen years as an amphibious scout for the advanced SEAL delivery system, he'd only his nose broken.

Over the years, he rose to the rank of petty officer and whenever he returned home, it was to march in the Memorial Day parade and talk to high school students about the advantages of enlisting in the military to further their education. Only his parents, brother and sister knew he was a SEAL, a fact he had withheld from Denise when they began dating but changed once they were married. He'd kept his role in the military a closely held secret because he feared family members could become possible targets for those seeking retaliation.

Within months of submitting his discharge papers, he had been approached by someone representing a private military freelancer, who'd offered to pay him as much in one month as what he'd earned in a year with the navy, and that included special incentive pay for hostile fire and dangerous duties. Again, he was unable to tell Denise where he was going or if he would come back, and in the end, she'd had enough. She walked out, dropped off Livia and Allison with his sister and gave Esther a note with a Texas address if he wanted to contact her. It had taken him a while to come to the realization that his wife had abandoned him and their children. When he finally contacted her, it was to send divorce papers. Much to his surprise, Denise signed the papers and relinquished her parental responsibility for her daughters. The final break coincided with his uncle's untimely death, and Aiden notified his employer that he would not be renewing his contract because he had to work for his family business. Fortunately, his mother had stepped in to help him care for her granddaughters until he was able to adjust to being a single father. His family had been there for him, and there wasn't anything Aiden wouldn't do to reciprocate in kind.

He swept the kitchen and storeroom, making certain not to leave any food for either four-legged or flying critters to feast on. He filled a pail with water and a strong industrial cleaner from the slop sink and mopped the kitchen. It was close to one in the morning when he changed his clothes and dropped the apron, tunic and pants in a bin with other soiled laundry; he set the alarm and got behind the wheel of his vehicle for the drive back home.

Aiden made a mental note to call a security company to wire his house. He wasn't as bothered with someone breaking in if the house wasn't occupied because whatever burglars took could be replaced. But now that Taryn was living there, and once his daughters returned, it would be three vulnerable people who could become possible targets if someone broke in when he worked nights.

He pulled into the driveway next to Taryn's SUV. The porch lights were on and so were the lights in the front of the house. "Good girl," Aiden whispered. Anyone passing by would surmise the occupants were still up.

Aiden unlocked the door and walked in the direction of Taryn's suite. The door was closed and no light came under the opening. It was apparent she had gone to bed. Turning on his heel, he made his way into the kitchen and opened a drawer under the countertop where he stored a directory of local businesses. He flipped the pages until he came to one advertising security systems, then something caught his attention. There was a note affixed to the door of the refrigerator with a Teacher's Rule red apple magnet.

He removed the note and left the magnet. His eyes quickly scanned the neat cursive:

Won't see you in the morning. Going to Charleston to shop, then having dinner with Jessica and

Sawyer. Hope you had a good night and an even better day tomorrow—Taryn.

Aiden smiled when he saw she'd added a smiley face. "Thank you," he said, smiling. He couldn't help but have a good day knowing she was around. He had found it so easy to talk to her without censoring himself, unlike with Denise. Aiden had never known when he opened his mouth whether or not it would send his ex into a tirade about something unrelated to their conversation.

He shook his head as if to rid his thoughts of his turbulent marriage. He'd done everything possible to make his ex-wife happy, but in the end, he realized there was nothing he could have done to make Denise happy. That was something she had to do on her own.

Aiden climbed the staircase to his attic retreat, stripped off his clothes and walked into the bathroom to shower. He smiled because his babies were coming home. He was excited to introduce them to the woman who would be responsible for opening up their young minds to the world around them and beyond.

His last thoughts before he fell asleep were of a beautiful woman who he hoped would share his home and family for the next year.

Taryn waved to Jessica as she alighted from her vehicle. "Happy New Year!"

Jessica Middleton hugged Taryn as if they hadn't seen one another in years when it had only been weeks. "Happy New Year to you, too. And welcome to Wickham Falls."

Taryn returned the hug. "Thank you." She pulled

back. "I never thought I'd say it, but I'm glad I moved down here."

"Now you know what I've been talking about," Jessica said, linking arms with Taryn and leading her up the porch to her house. "At first, I experienced culture shock moving from DC, but now I know it's the best decision I've ever made."

"I suppose it's not really culture shock for me because I knew what to expect," Taryn admitted. Her prior visits had given her a glimpse of a region that resembled a folk art painting depicting small-town Americana. "Where's Bootsy?" She had expected the dog to coming running to greet her.

"Sawyer and Bootsy are in New York for the weekend. Come inside," Jessica said as she led the way into the house.

She stopped and stared at her friend. The pixie cut was perfect for Jessica's round brown face. Her large dark eyes, button-like nose and generously curved lips reminded Taryn of one of her childhood dolls. "And you didn't go with them?" Taryn knew Sawyer's software company was based in New York City.

"No. Sawyer got a text this morning, asking him to come for an emergency board meeting, and he decided to take his furry best friend with him. He told me his partners are going to revisit whether to take their company public."

Taryn followed Jessica into the kitchen. "Have they set a date to announce the IPO if they do decide to go public?"

"Sawyer said it probably wouldn't happen until May."

Taryn was aware that Jessica's husband had hinted about selling his share in Enigma4For4 if or when the company went public. "If that happens, then everything will change for you guys. Wickham Falls' youngest millionaires will probably become billionaires and even Bootsy will become a target for dognappers who'll hold my pet-nephew hostage for a million-dollar ransom."

Jessica bit her lip to keep from laughing. "Where do you come up with these scenarios?"

"I don't know. They just pop into my head. On a more serious note, people around here will look at you and Sawyer differently once the news gets out."

"I know that," Jessica admitted. "Folks know that Sawyer has done very well for himself as a software engineer, but they really don't know how much he's worth. What I don't want is for us to become pseudo-celebrities."

"That's only going to happen if you build some monstrosity of a gated mansion with garages filled with Bentleys and Lamborghinis."

"That will never happen. I told Sawyer I plan to die in this house. We have enough bedrooms, even if we decide to have two or three kids. We have more than an acre, which means there's a lot of space for children to run and play."

Taryn sat on a stool at the cooking island, watching Jessica slice shiitake mushrooms, shallots and a carrot. She was making one of Taryn's favorite dishes: chicken and biscuits. "You guys will be like Warren Buffet, who still lives in the first house he ever bought."

"Between this place and Sawyer's Manhattan loft, we're set when it comes to owning properties." Jessica put down the knife. "Enough talk about me and Sawyer. How are you getting along with Aiden?"

Taryn paused, staring up at the shiny copper pots

and pans suspended on a rack above the cooking island. "We're getting along well."

Jessica lifted questioning eyebrows. "I know you were reluctant to live with a man again after how that cheating idiot treated you, but I'm glad you changed your mind."

"I'm sharing the house with Aiden and his children, and that's a lot different than living with him."

"Have you met his daughters?"

"Not yet. They're still in Florida."

"When are they coming back?" Jessica asked.

"Sunday. I'll give them a couple of days to reconnect with their father before I begin working with them."

"How long has it been since you've been involved with preschoolers?"

"At least six years," Taryn confirmed. She'd taught pre-K, kindergarten, and second and third grade. "I really prefer teaching third-graders."

"I'm with you. Initially, I was upset when told I would teach fifth grade, but I've come to enjoy the older kids."

Taryn rested her elbows on the countertop. "How is it to go to work and come home with your husband?"

Jessica walked over to the refrigerator, removed a container with a rotisserie chicken, a plastic bag of frozen baby peas, a bottle of milk and cradling them to her chest, returned to the cooking island. "We actually don't leave the house at the same time. He goes in before seven because he has to make certain the computers in the tech lab are working before his eight o'clock computer programming class. And he usually gets home before me because he's assigned to the high school and their dismissal is at two. What I really like is that he always starts dinner, so by the time I get home, all I have to do is make the sides."

"I forgot that your man knows how to cook," Taryn teased.

"Sawyer is a neophyte compared to Aiden. The last time we ate at the Wolf Den, he made braised lamb shanks that were to die for. I know you're going to enjoy living in his house with him cooking for you."

Initially, she had been apprehensive about living in the same house as her employer, but there was something about Aiden's easygoing manner that put her immediately at ease. "He *is* the real deal when it comes to cooking. When I asked why he hadn't gone to culinary school he said it would've been a waste because the Den's regulars want comfort food, not fancy dishes with names they can't pronounce."

"He's right, Taryn. Remember when we lived in DC and saved enough money to go to that fancy French restaurant everyone was raving about?"

"I'd love to forget. We just looked at each other when the waiter set our plates on the table with one baby carrot, three roasted brussels sprouts and a filet so small we could eat it in two bites."

"And I couldn't help laughing when you said, 'Hell no! We are not paying ninety dollars for this itty-bitty food!'"

Taryn had put aside money she had earned babysitting so she and Jessica could dress up and eat at a restaurant that had tablecloths and reported impeccable service. Most times, they shopped at the local supermarket and prepared their own meals. If they did eat out, it was at local barbecue or chicken joints offering student discounts and because they were able to get a lot more food for their money.

Jessica made a sucking sound with her tongue and teeth. "And they had the audacity to indicate a suggested gratuity. If I'd known we were going to get a dieter's plate, I never would've ordered that glass of wine."

"Word," Taryn drawled. "The money we paid for two glasses of wine we could've gone to the local liquor store and bought two or maybe even three bottles if they were on sale. You just reminded me of something when you mentioned wine. I drove up to Charleston this morning to do some shopping. I stopped in a store advertising wine tasting and ordered a couple of cases of your favorite rosé. The shopkeeper didn't have them in stock but promised he will ship them to you next week."

Slipping on a pair of disposable gloves, Jessica shredded the chicken. "You didn't have to do that."

"Consider it my contribution to our girls' night out."

"I enjoy our girls' nights, but it's our college days I treasure most." There was a wistful tone in Jessica's voice. "Even though we didn't have much, we had some very good times."

Taryn nodded. "I have to agree with you. Before you came to Howard my father deposited enough in my checking account to cover rent and buy enough food to last to the next month. My first semester I'd run out of money by the third week and my diet consisted of ramen noodles for breakfast, lunch and dinner. When you transferred to Howard in our junior year, I was a pro when it came to sticking to a budget. Daddy said if I wanted to hang out or go to concerts, then I was on my own. It wasn't that my parents couldn't afford to give me an extra fifty or hundred dollars every other month for entertainment or recreation. It's just that they wanted me to understand that if I want more than the basic necessities, then I'd have to work for it. That's why I agreed to babysit and tutor the McKees' kids. My parents were willing to pay for my undergraduate studies, but if I wanted a graduate degree, then I was on my own."

"We were both lucky to get teaching positions while we were in grad school," Jessica said, as she melted butter in a large enameled cast-iron casserole before adding the shallots, mushrooms and carrot chunks.

Jessica was right. They'd been hired within weeks of graduating Howard. "That's because crime in that neighborhood was so bad the district had a hard time hiring and retaining teachers. I don't know if I told you that a second-grader in my school had a reputation for hitting teachers. Little Boo, that was what everyone called him, came over to me and raised his little hand and announced in front of the class in a Barry White baritone that he was going to smack me. I managed to keep a straight face when I said, 'What if I smack you back?' Of course, he didn't know I'd never strike a child, but I must have gotten through to Little Boo because he sat his little pissy behind down and never got up in my class again."

Jessica laughed so hard she could hardly catch her breath. "Was he really pissy?" she asked once she recovered.

"Yeah! He'd wait until he'd have to go to the bathroom to tell me he had to go. By that time, it was too late and he'd end up wetting his pants. Every day his mother would have to bring him a change of clothes.

I had to bite my tongue when I wanted to tell her he needed pull-ups."

Taryn and Jessica laughed uncontrollably when they recalled the antics of some of their former students. "I've got you when it comes to the parents," she boasted. "I've had a few who got in my face because of the grades and comments on their child's report card."

Jessica's hands stilled. "What did you do?"

"I'd give them my best death-stare and once they realized I wasn't a punk, they'd back down. Meanwhile, my heart was beating so fast I feared they could hear it. But I knew if I didn't stand my ground, I'd have to hire a bodyguard to drop me off and take me home."

"Imagine if you'd shown up with Aiden. I bet you would've heard crickets. Speaking of Aiden," Jessica continued without taking a breath. "Are you committed to teaching his daughters for the next two years?"

"No. I told him I wanted a one-year commitment, and if things work out, then I'd commit to another year. His oldest daughter just turned five, so she won't be eligible to enter first grade until next August."

Jessica gave Taryn a prolonged stare. "He's going to have to make a choice whether to homeschool them himself if he doesn't want them to go the public school or send them to a private school."

"You're right. Either that or marry someone willing to homeschool them until they're ready for middle school."

"From what I've heard about his ex-wife, I don't think Aiden's too anxious to marry again," Jessica said.

Now Taryn's curiosity was piqued. "Did you know his ex?"

"Not personally, but rumors were swirling that she

had cheated on her husband. At that time, I hadn't met Aiden, so to me it was just hearsay. There's one thing you'll have to get used to living in a small town."

"What's that?" Taryn asked.

"Gossip. That folks will talk about you and Aiden sleeping together."

"We're not sleeping together and I have no intention of sharing a bed with Aiden."

Reaching across the space separating them, Jessica grasped Taryn's hand. "Don't sweat it, Taryn. They talked about me and Sawyer until we were married."

"It turned out well for you and Sawyer because *you are* married. The difference is I'm not going to marry Aiden."

Chapter Six

Aiden, waiting at baggage claim, watched his daughters' approach, accompanied by an airline employee. He smiled when seeing the identification tags around their necks. It was the first time Allison and Livia had been on a plane, and the experience was even more momentous for them because they'd flown alone.

A smile parted his lips when he returned Livia's wave. In the eight weeks since he'd last seen his children, they'd changed. Both were tanned, Allison was taller and the sun had lightened Livia's hair from dirty-blond to flaxen.

"That's my daddy," Allison told the man holding her hand.

Reaching into the pocket of his jeans, Aiden removed his driver's license and handed it to the attendant, who checked it with the information on the form Ruby Shepherd had completed for her granddaughters.

"Just sign here, Mr. Gibson."

Aiden scrawled his signature on the form relinquishing the airline of all liability for transporting his children. "Thank you." Reaching for the phone in the pocket of his jacket, he sent his mother a text message that her granddaughters had arrived safely.

He put away the phone, and bending slightly, he picked up both girls and landed loud kisses on their cheeks. "Welcome home, princesses."

Livia hugged his neck. "We saw a lot of princesses in Florida, Daddy."

Allison also looped her arms around his neck. His dark-haired, dark-eyed daughter was a constant reminder of the woman with whom he'd fallen in love, married and eventually divorced. Allison may have inherited her mother's looks, but fortunately not her personality. If Livia was a free spirit, then her older sister was an old spirit. His first-born reminded him of someone much too wise for her tender years.

"When are we going to meet our teacher, Daddy?" Allison asked.

Aiden kissed her hair. "You'll meet her as soon as I get you home."

"Let's go!" Livia shouted.

He carried his daughters out of the terminal to the parking lot. The girls never traveled with baggage because his mother made certain to have clothes for them to wear. Ruby always drove up from Orlando to pick up her granddaughters and usually spent a few days in The Falls reconnecting with family before getting back on the road and completing the six-hundred-and-fifty-mile trip in ten hours.

Aiden hadn't had much contact with Taryn because

he was on the night shift. She was in bed when he arrived home and up and out of the house when he woke. Aside from when she left the note indicating she was going to Charleston and subsequently eating with Sawyer and Jessica, they were like ships passing in the night.

"Drive faster, Daddy," Livia urged from the back seat. "I want to meet my teacher."

"Yeah, Daddy," Allison chimed in. "We want to meet our teacher."

He glanced up at the rearview mirror. "If I drive any faster, the police will stop me and give us a ticket. Do you guys have money to pay the fine?"

Livia lifted her shoulders, while Allison extended her hands, palms up. "We don't have money," they said in unison.

Aiden smiled. "If you don't have any money, then you can't expect me to drive faster."

"We don't have money, but you do," Allison said.

"I work hard and make money to take care of you two munchkins. I buy your clothes, food, pay for Grandma to drive you to Florida and bring you back. I also have to pay the electric company so we have lights and the gas company for cooking and heating. Do you want to live in a house with no lights and heat, especially in the winter?"

"No," they chorused again.

"If that's the case, then I'm not going to drive any faster than the speed limit. You will get to meet Miss Taryn once we get home."

Aiden did not like talking about money with his children because the topic had been a source of contention between him and their mother. He'd deposited money into an account for her to use to pay bills, run the household and have enough left for her to buy something extra for herself. However, whenever he returned home he found letters with past due notices for credit card bills and companies threatening to disconnect the phone, cable, electricity and gas. When he confronted Denise, her excuse was she forgot. She may have forgotten to send the checks, while she could not explain what she'd done with the money she'd withdrawn from the bank account.

Aiden realized he had to assume full responsibility for paying the bills. So he opened another account, went online and set up a direct payment schedule. Denise had a meltdown once she realized the monies in her checking account had been drastically reduced by ninety percent. It was only when one of her deadbeat brothers came to the house screaming at his sister that she'd promised him money because he was facing jail time for back child support that he realized she had been subsidizing her family.

The man's desperation was evident when he threatened Aiden, who'd ordered him to get off his property. Rather than a physical confrontation, which would have resulted in serious injury to his brother-in-law, Aiden called the sheriff's office and had him forcibly removed. The first time he realized there was a serious crack in his marriage was when Denise left that night to stay with her parents. She returned two days later, smiling and laughing as if nothing had happened with the news that she was pregnant with their first child.

There were times when he did not recognize the woman with whom he'd fallen in love and married. Within months of exchanging vows she'd changed from being fun-loving and affectionate to sullen and argumentative. And whenever he'd asked her what was bothering her her response had been "nothing." Denise's dark moods would last for several days to a week before they vanished like magic.

"Daddy, are we really going to have school in our house?" Allison asked, breaking into his thoughts.

"Yes." He didn't tell his daughters that what they would experience with Taryn would be a combination of childcare and an introduction to a formal education. They would be socialized and educated at the same time.

Livia shared a smile with her sister. "Will Allie and me have a desk?"

"Yes, Livia. You'll both have your own desk."

Aiden smiled to himself as the two girls chatted excitedly about what they wanted to do in school. They'd heard their older cousins talk about school, and Livia and Allison said they couldn't wait to join them. Aiden hadn't had the heart to tell them that wasn't going to happen. It wasn't until he'd come up with the notion of hiring a live-in nanny that he'd gone online and researched the job description. That's when he realized they were more caregivers than educators.

"Daddy?"

"What is it, Allie?"

"Can we go to Ruthie's today?"

Aiden had planned to prepare a traditional Sunday dinner and catch up on what his daughters had done and seen while in Florida. "Is that really what you want?"

"Yes."

"Of course, Daddy," Livia chimed in.

"Okay. Then Ruthie's it is. But first you're going to have to change because what you're wearing isn't warm enough." They'd come back wearing T-shirts, shorts, hoodies and sandals.

"But it was so hot in Florida," Allison said. "We went swimming every day in Grandma and Grandpa's pool."

"Oh, my gosh! You can swim?" Aiden asked, teasingly.

Allison gasped. "Of course we can swim. You taught us."

Aiden slapped his forehead with the heel of his hand. "I'm sorry. I forgot."

He loved teasing his girls, if only to keep them on their toes. He'd taught them to swim before they were two. Whenever he was home on an extended leave he would take them to a pool in a sports club in a nearby town and give them lessons where they'd taken to the water like ducks. Once they were proficient enough to swim without floaties, he'd cautioned them never to swim without having an adult present.

"Daddy?"

"Yes, Livia."

"Can we have a pool like Grandma and Grandpa? That way we can swim in the backyard instead of going to that place where the pool is so crowded and we always get splashed."

Aiden signaled and maneuvered off the turnpike and onto Route 77, heading south toward Beckley. "I'll think about it."

"You always say that," Livia and Allison said in unison.

"Do you always have to say the same thing?" he countered, smiling. It was as if the girls were twins and could read each other's thoughts.

"We don't say the same thing," Allison said in defense of her younger sister.

"Daddy, the pool," Livia whined.

Aiden clenched his teeth. Once his kids latched onto something, they were like dogs with a bone. They refused to let it go until he told them in no uncertain terms that he refused to do or give them whatever they wanted. Putting in a pool was an additional expense, which would further deplete the money he had set aside for their college education. Livia and Allison attending college had become a priority because he had forfeited the privilege when he enlisted in the navy rather than accepting an athletic scholarship.

As a high school student with above-average grades, he had been more than just a jock. He'd planned to attend college not because of his parents but because he'd wanted to leave Wickham Falls and see the world. When he'd made a list of colleges he wanted to attend, most were on the West Coast. It was as if it was calling him to come and lie on the beach, surf in the ocean and take in the stunning vistas when driving along US Route 101. Much to his delight he got his fervent wish to see California when he stepped foot on Coronado Island for BUD/S training.

"I told you I'd think about, so let's not talk about it again." There was an edge to his voice that Livia and Allison were familiar with, as the sisters looked at each other and fell into a chastised silence.

There had been a time when Aiden had talked to Denise about putting in an inground pool, but in the end, he agreed to renovate the house to accommodate their rapidly expanding family. Aiden had been shocked when he'd come home after working with several other security contractors training soldiers and reorganizing militaries in Nigeria to the news that he was to become a father again. Nearly two months after giving birth to Allison, Denise was pregnant again, despite their having used protection. Knowing he had another mouth to feed, he signed up for another year with the security company. One year led to two, then three, until his uncle passed away and Aiden was forced to walk away from everything military and take his place at home to keep the family business viable.

What he could not understand was Denise's complaint that she didn't see him enough when he was active navy, then when he was a private military contractor and then as a cook at the Wolf Den. In the end, he realized even if he spent every waking hour of the day with her, Denise still would've found something in which to murmur about. After a while, he gave up trying to appease her and concentrated on his children.

"Grandma is getting a new dog," Allison said after Aiden had driven several miles.

"When did she decide this?" he asked. The last time he'd spoken to his mother, she hadn't mentioned getting a pet.

"She told us when she was driving us to the airport."

"She said she would have it when we come down again," Livia chimed in.

Aiden flipped his directional signal and headed to the local road leading to Wickham Falls. "Did she say what kind of dog she was getting?" His daughters had been begging for a dog for a while, but he was reluctant to get them one because he would be the one taking care of the animal. And his hours were too erratic to give the dog the attention it deserved.

"No," Allison said. "We told her it can't be too big or we can't walk it. Grandma also said we are old enough to have our own dog."

"Grandmas tell their grandbabies what they want to hear," Aiden said under his breath.

"What did you say, Daddy?" Allison asked.

"Nothing," he lied. "I was just talking to myself." Aiden made a mental note to talk to his mother before she suggested he take on more responsibility like taking care of a dog.

He remembered telling Taryn, *The only thing I'm going to say about my children is that they're going to prove to be quite a challenge.* And he hadn't lied to her. His daughters were curious, loquacious, stubborn *and* resolute. Yet instinct told him Taryn was up to the task but he would find out soon enough in about ten minutes.

Taryn opened the front door at the sound of an approaching vehicle. Aiden had left the house after breakfast when he received an alert on his phone that the flight carrying his daughters was scheduled to arrive on time. He had invited her to accompany him, but she declined. Perhaps there were things his children wanted to tell him that she didn't need to be privy to.

Although she'd settled into what would be her home for the next eleven months, Taryn had looked forward to their return because she'd begun to feel uncomfortable with Aiden whenever they sat down to eat together; she'd look up and find him staring at her. And when she'd return his stare, he wouldn't bother to look away. The one time she'd asked why he was staring, he said she reminded him of someone he'd seen before but couldn't remember where. She had not believed him.

As a former highly trained and elite commando, he'd been tested physically and mentally and Taryn doubted he'd forget anyone or anything he'd seen.

He'd taken her advice and had the property secured with cameras and motion detectors that were monitored on his cell phone. Aiden gave her the code, and she hadn't realized how much safer she felt whenever she armed the system before retiring for bed when he worked late.

She knew what Livia and Allison looked like from the photographs lining the living room mantelpiece. What Taryn found off was that there were no photos of them with their mother. It was as if Aiden had tried to exorcise his daughters' mother out of their lives.

Walking out onto the porch, she smiled when Aiden got out and waved before opening the rear door. A little girl with ash-blond waves emerged first, followed by her sister with a profusion of dark curls cascading around her face. They raced up the porch steps, and then stopped short as if stopped by a bungee cord when they noticed her. A pair each of large green and dark brown eyes met hers, as they seemed to withdraw without moving. Aiden slowly mounted the steps, his hands cradling his daughters at his side. "Allie, Livia, this is Miss Taryn. She's going to be your new teacher."

Taryn came down several steps and bent down until her head was even with theirs. "I've been waiting to meet you." Her voice was soft and coaxing, as she hoped to put them at ease. She smiled at the brunette with soulful brown eyes. "I know that you're Allison."

Allison blinked, long dark lashes touching her tanned cheeks. "How do you know that?"

"Because I saw a picture of you in the house."

"Who told you my name?"

"Your father." Her answer seemed to satisfy the child as she nodded. "And, of course, you're Livia," Taryn said, looking into the green eyes that appeared much too wise for a child her age. It was then she recalled Aiden had called Livia a free spirit, which meant she could possibly question her teachings. As long as she knew what she was facing, then Taryn knew how to proceed accordingly.

"How long are you going to be our teacher?" Livia asked.

Aiden patted Livia's head. "Enough questions. Let's go inside and I'll explain everything."

"Do you ever wear a coat?" Taryn whispered to Aiden after the two girls ran into the house. He wore a pullover sweater with his jeans and boots.

"Why?"

"Because I wouldn't want you to get sick."

He winked at her. "I didn't know you cared. And I hardly ever get sick. Most of the time, I'm going from the house to the SUV or from the SUV to the restaurant."

She gave him a sidelong glance. "Okay, Superman."

"I'd rather be Batman."

"What's the matter, you don't like red tights?"

"Not more than a cape and cowl. Of all of the DC Comics characters, Batman is my favorite."

"Have you ever attended Comic-Con?"

Aiden flashed a sheepish grin. "No, but it is on my bucket list."

Excitable screams came from the rear of the house and Taryn and Aiden looked at each other and shared a smile. "I bet they saw the classroom," she said.

"Let's go see."

Taryn wished she'd had her phone so she could have taken a picture of Allison and Livia's faces. They were shrieking and jumping up and down at the same time.

Allison ran over to the desk with her name. "Daddy, is this really my desk?"

"Yes, it is. This is your classroom and Miss Taryn is your teacher."

Taryn was glad that Aiden had referred to her as Miss Taryn rather than Miss Robinson. She found that younger children were more apt to remember a teacher's first name rather than a surname.

Livia walked slowly over to her desk and sat down. "I love my desk."

Allison turned to look at Aiden. "Is this really our classroom, Daddy?"

"Yes, it is. You'll get a chance to look at everything later. Now it's time to change your clothes if you still want to go to Ruthie's."

The two girls jumped up like jack-in-the-boxes and raced out of the classroom. Taryn and Aiden shared a knowing smile. "There's no doubt they approve."

He nodded. "I'd be shocked if they didn't. You did an incredible job."

Taryn inclined her head. "Thank you."

"The girls want me to take them to Ruthie's. Are you coming with us?"

"Are you inviting me?"

"Of course."

He was her boss and his children were her students, and Taryn had no intention of blurring or crossing the line from professional to personal.

Accompanying Aiden to the Wolf Den was necessary for him to introduce her to his family, but going with him and his children to a local restaurant would elicit the gossip Jessica had warned her about. "Do you mind if I ask for a raincheck? Your children just got back and you need to reconnect with them without my tagging along."

Aiden saw indecision in Taryn's expression. "What's bothering you?"

"Why do you think something's bothering me?"

"Because you're biting on your lip. I've noticed you doing that whenever you have to think of a response."

Her lips trembled as she tried not to smile. "So you think you know me that well?"

"Well enough. You've been here less than a week, and although we haven't spent much time together, I've watched you closely and there are times when your face is an open book."

Her eyebrows lifted questioningly. "I'm that transparent?"

"Sometimes. You think people are going to talk when they see you with me and my girls. Please let me finish," Aiden said when Taryn opened her mouth. "If that's what you think, then you're right. Since my divorce, no one has ever seen me with another woman—without or without my children."

She squinted at Aiden. "Are you saying you don't care what they say about you?"

"I'm beyond caring because I can't change what people think. And whatever I say or do will not change their minds. You're going to be here for the next eleven months and that means it's about time folks get used to seeing you with me, Livia, and Allie. As soon as the girls change, we'll head on over because Ruthie's is always crowded on Sundays and we'll have to wait for a table."

He just gave me a flippin' order. Aiden had gone from asking her to go with him to Ruthie's to ordering her to go. She wanted to refuse but knew it wasn't in her best interest to become insubordinate, while she had to constantly remind herself that Aiden was her employer.

"Should I genuflect in acquiescence or salute you?"

Aiden stared at her as if she'd spoken a language he couldn't understand. "You're really something," he said after a pregnant pause.

"What are you talking about?" Her expression radiated innocence.

He shook his head. "Forget it. Please be ready to leave once Allie and Livia come down."

Gotcha! Taryn knew she'd gotten the best of Aiden without outwardly challenging his authority. Turning on her heel, she headed for her bedroom to get a coat. Her shopping trip to Charleston had been highly successful when she purchased items to put her personal touch on the suite and adjoining bathroom. Silver frames held family photographs and a quartet of moth orchids in hand-painted pots doubled as a centerpiece on the table in the sitting area. She had also purchased a cashmere throw to ward off the chill while viewing the television after she lowered the thermostat. Whenever she slept in a heated bedroom, Taryn always woke with a dry nose and throat.

More potted plants and candles lined the ledge of the sunken tub under one of the two skylights in the bathroom. She'd discovered a collection of cut-glass apothecary jars in an antique shop and couldn't resist purchasing six. Three she filled with cotton balls, cotton swabs and cleansing pads, while colorful glass beads, tiny white seashells and dried herbs found a home in the remaining three.

Taryn decided not to change her jeans and sweater to something a little less casual. Ruthie's was an all-you-can-eat buffet restaurant catering to families. She selected a waist-length wool jacket and retraced her steps. She'd just entered the kitchen when she was met with Livia crying and stomping her bare feet. The little girl had changed into a pink tank top, black tights and a pink sequined tutu.

Allison, holding on to Aiden's hand, pointed at her sister with her free hand. "Daddy, make her take it off! We are not playing fairies now!"

Aiden closed his eyes and inhaled. "Livia, we can't go until you wear something else."

Livia pushed out her lips. "But I want to wear it!"

When it looked at as if the situation was going to end in a stalemate, Taryn decided to put her training to the test as a teacher who'd had to mediate countless situations involving her students. She left her coat on the stool at the cooking island, walked over to Livia and took her hand.

"Do you want me to play fairies with you after we eat?"

The tears in the green eyes had turned them into pools of polished emeralds. Her tiny chin quivered when she stared up at Taryn. "Will you?"

Taryn smiled. "I promise. And I always keep my promises. Now, let's go upstairs and change and when we come back, I promise to read you a story about fairies while you wear your fairy clothes."

Livia sniffled. "Okay."

"We'll be right back," Taryn said to Aiden and Allison.

They left the kitchen and took the back staircase to Livia's bedroom. Taryn was shocked when she saw dresser drawers open and clothes spilling out and on the floor. It looked as if a whirlwind had blown through the room.

She didn't know if Aiden's daughters were taught to pick up after themselves, but Taryn knew if it continued, then they were certain to become messy teenagers. "You need a T-shirt and jeans."

Livia sat on the floor and stripped down to her panties and tank top. Taryn watched as she found a long-sleeved T-shirt with a colorful Disney character on it and a pair of jeans. She was able to dress herself without assistance. Taryn found a drawer with socks and handed them to the child. Fifteen minutes later, they descended the staircase and walked into the kitchen. She'd brushed Livia's hair and styled it in a single braid under a colorful knitted cap. Livia didn't want to wear a coat and only relented when Taryn threatened not to play fairies with her.

Aiden had remarked that his children were challenging and she saw firsthand how truthful he had been. Free-spirited and I-want-to-do-whatever-I-want Livia Gibson was going to be more of a challenge for Taryn than her elder sister.

Livia skipped over to her father. "I'm ready to go now, Daddy."

Reaching for Taryn's coat, he held it as she slipped her arms into the sleeves. "Thank you," he whispered in her ear.

"There's no need to thank me. I'm used to hissy

fits, temper tantrums and kiddie meltdowns," she said sotto voce.

Aiden pressed his mouth to her hair. "I still thank you."

"Let's go, Daddy," the two girls chorused.

Aiden gathered his keys off the countertop as everyone filed out of the house. He armed the security system and then closed and locked the door. Taryn had opened the rear door to the Suburban and made certain Livia and Allison were belted in when he joined them.

He opened the passenger-side door and assisted Taryn up before rounding the SUV to take his seat behind the wheel. "Is everyone seated and belted in before we take off?" he questioned loudly.

"I like flying, Daddy," Allison said from the rear seat.

"Me, too," said her sister.

Aiden tapped the start-engine button. "Maybe the next time you visit your grandparents you'll fly down instead of Grandma and Grandpa driving up to get you."

Pressing her head against the headrest, Taryn closed her eyes and listened to the conversation between Aiden and his daughters.

"Miss Taryn, do you like Ruthie's?" Allison asked.

"Yes, I do." Jessica had taken her to the restaurant during her first trip to Wickham Falls.

"What do you like to eat?"

Taryn rose slightly in her seat and smiled at Allison. "Everything."

"You can't eat everything," Livia piped up. "There's too much food."

Aiden patted Taryn's knee over her jeans. "You have

to monitor everything you say around Miss Mouth Almighty," he said under his breath.

"Word!"

Smiling, Aiden turned into the restaurant parking lot and maneuvered into an empty space. "It looks as if we've come at the right time. The lot isn't full."

Chapter Seven

Aiden watched Taryn closely for her reaction to those staring at her seated at the table with him and his daughters. She could've earned an award for acting when she ignored the stares and finger pointing as she listened intently to his daughters talking about what they'd seen and done in Orlando. He also noticed that whenever interacting with Livia and Allison her voice changed so it was softer and calming.

Allison excitedly told her about seeing an alligator sunning on a rock in a park, while Livia had been transfixed by flocks of flamingoes and egrets that had gathered to feed in a shallow lake. "There were so many birds they covered the sky, Miss Taryn."

Taryn's expression mirrored shock. "Wow! That must have been something to see."

"It was," Livia confirmed as she picked up a Tater

Tot, dipping it in a glob of ketchup before popping it into her mouth.

"Do you like the chicken and waffles?" Aiden asked Taryn.

She smiled at him. "It's delicious." Taryn pointed to his plate of coleslaw and salmon patties with a lemon-cheese sauce. "The salmon croquettes?"

"Delicious. It's been a while since I've made salmon croquettes."

Aiden wanted to tell Taryn it's been a while since he'd done a lot of things he liked. However, that would change now that she was here. Whenever he was home he'd always set aside Sundays as family day. It was his day to get up early and prepare a monstrous breakfast. After everyone had eaten their fill, they would climb back into bed together to watch cartoons and would all invariably fall asleep.

Summer Sundays were devoted to visiting state and county fairs; fall Sundays were for pumpkin and apple picking, as well as for raking and bagging leaves. During the winter months, they pretended they were pioneers, pitching a tent in the living room and cooking their meals in the fireplace. Making family Sunday special could not make up for the times he'd spent away from home, but it was an attempt to create lasting memories for his children.

"Daddy, can Livia and me have ice cream if we finish our food?"

Aiden blinked as if coming out of a trance. He stared at Allison, marveling that with each passing birthday she looked more and more like her mother. There had been something about Denise's dark hair and dark eyes that he hadn't been able to resist.

"Yes, you may."

Aiden's pet peeve was wasting food, and he'd brought Allison and Livia to the Den to show them the food the restaurant donated to the local soup kitchen. He knew they were probably too young to comprehend that kids their age went to bed hungry because there was no food in their homes, yet he'd wanted to make them aware of how lucky they were.

"Can I get it by myself?" Livia asked.

"Grandma lets us get our own ice cream," Allison said, agreeing with her sister.

Taryn touched her napkin to the corners of her mouth. "Let's go get ice cream together."

Aiden wanted to hug and kiss Taryn for suggesting she go with his daughters. The dessert section was on the other side of the restaurant. He wasn't paranoid, yet he was reluctant to let his children out of his range of vision whenever they were in public. There were too many stories about children who went missing in supermarkets and department stores. He nodded to Taryn and she acknowledged him with a nod of her own.

Taryn waited for Aiden to disarm the alarm before entering the house. She chided herself for having soft-serve ice cream with strawberry syrup, walnuts, whipped cream and a cherry. Although it was early afternoon, she was ready for a nap.

It appeared she wasn't the only drowsy one, when Livia yawned and said, "I'm sleepy, Daddy."

Aiden took her coat and then Allison's. "That's because Grandma got you guys up early to catch your flight. Go upstairs, take off your clothes and don't forget to wash your face and hands before you go to bed."

Allison narrowed her eyes at her father. "Was that la-dinner, Daddy?"

Aiden shared a look with Taryn, as she struggled not to laugh. "No, baby. It was lunch. I'll make dinner later."

Taryn slipped off her coat, handing it to Aiden, then reached for Livia's hand. "I'll take you upstairs for your nap."

Livia glanced up at her. "Are you going to take a nap with me?"

"No, sweetie. I'll stay with you until you fall asleep. Then I'm going to my bedroom to take my nap."

Her explanation seemed to satisfy Livia, who wrested her hand from Taryn's loose hold, raced up the staircase and into her bedroom. Taryn stood in the doorway to the connecting bathroom as the sisters washed their hands and faces in the double vanity. She groaned inwardly when they stripped off their street clothes and left them on the bathroom floor. She planned to incorporate socialization into her lesson plans, and Taryn would begin with her students picking up after themselves.

Taryn sat on the window seat, waiting and watching Livia tossing restlessly until she finally fell asleep. Then, she began picking up articles of clothing, folding them neatly and putting them away. She repeated the action in Allison's bedroom. When Aiden had given her a tour of his home, there hadn't been any evidence of clothes strewn on the floor in any room in the house. Had he, she wondered, picked up after his daughters, or had he relegated that responsibility to the cleaning service?

She found Aiden in the kitchen trussing a roasting chicken. The distinctive fragrance of rosemary permeated the air. He'd tuned a radio on the countertop to a station featuring soft jazz. "They're down for the count."

He smiled at her when she sat on the stool, watching him. "That's a first. I can't remember the last time they napped in the afternoon."

Taryn knew she had to broach the subject of his daughters' sloppiness. Yet she didn't want to contradict his vision as to how he wanted to raise his children. "I noticed that Livia and Allison leave their clothes on the floor."

Aiden finished securing the bird's legs with butcher twine. "They picked up that habit from my sister's daughters. And when I mention it to Esther, she claims they'll outgrow it."

"Do you really believe that, Aiden?"

"No. But I don't know what to do about it."

"Do you mind if I try?"

Aiden washed his hands and dried them on a dish towel before covering the roaster with foil and setting the pan on a shelf in the refrigerator. "You have my permission to do whatever is necessary to improve their lives. I can't argue with my sister about how she's raising her kids, because I need her to watch Livia and Allie when I work nights. I don't even attempt to get involved with my mother because she's quick to tell me it's a grandmother's prerogative to spoil her grandchildren."

"She sounds like my mother. Mildred Robinson will rest her hands at her waist and dare anyone to say a word when she chooses to give her grandbabies whatever they ask for, and that irks the heck of out my sister-in-law."

"How many grandchildren does your mother have?"

"Three. Two boys and a girl."

"Has she been on your case to give her another grandchild?" Aiden asked.

Resting her chin on her hand, Taryn's mouth curved into an unconscious smile. "She'll drop hints every once in a while."

"It doesn't bother you?"

"No. What about you, Aiden. Do you think you would ever marry again?"

He laughed softly. "I guess I left myself wide open for that."

"Well?"

"Maybe one of these days when my girls are older."

"How old, Aiden?" Taryn asked. "When they're ready to make you a grandfather?"

Aiden affected a screw-face. "Very funny."

"I'm not trying to be funny. You have to have a time-frame when you'd like to marry again."

Aiden walked around the cooking island and sat next to Taryn. "I'll marry when you marry."

Taryn blinked slowly. Aiden was so close she could feel his warm, moist breath on her cheek. "That may not be for a long time."

"It's the same with me. I did say when my girls were older."

"Will you send me an invitation to your wedding?"

Aiden tugged on the end of her ponytail. "Of course."

"Speaking of your daughters, have you thought about taking them to the annual Father/Daughter Dance? This year's theme is a magical forest with fairies, elves, leprechauns and gnomes. And you know how much Livia loves fairies."

Aiden recalled his sister's excitement when their father had escorted her to the dance that was held in the high school gym. Many years ago, the school board had presented the idea to the town council of an event in which all Wickham Falls fathers honored their daughters, because female students had been complaining about the dearth of school-related activities in which they could participate. The council approved the event, along with support from local businesses. "Who told you about the Father/Daughter Dance?"

"Jessica. She's volunteered to be a chaperone this year. She also said there are prizes for the best costumes. If you decide to take Livia and Allison, I'm willing to make their costumes."

Aiden shook his head. "It's something I haven't considered."

"Why not? Don't you think it would be fun for them? There will be games along with dancing."

"I'm sure it would be fun, but I don't dance."

Taryn slowly shook her head. "Are you saying that you've never danced?"

"Yes, ma'am."

"Do you want to learn?"

"Why? Are you going to teach me?" Aiden asked glibly.

"That I am. You have almost two months to turn your two left feet into a right and left. I doubt if they're going to play a lot of slow tunes, so we're going to concentrate on the upbeat ones."

"It's not going to happen."

Taryn slipped off the stool. "Because you say so? If you can survive BUD/S and Hell Week, then you can learn to dance."

Aiden stared at Taryn's hips in the jeans that showed off her slender curves when she walked over to the radio and selected a station to one featuring slow tunes. He'd constantly reminded himself that Taryn was off-limits, and he had to be very, very careful not to blur lines, because, after all, he was her employer.

Allison had asked him last year if they were going to the dance because her cousins were going and he'd made up an excuse why he couldn't take her. He hadn't trusted himself when it came to encountering some of the girls who'd refused to play with his daughters because of what they'd heard their parents say. Aiden wouldn't have confronted the girls but their fathers, and he knew the confrontation would not have ended amicably.

And he knew the subject would come up again with Livia and Allison once his nieces mentioned they were going to the dance with their father. Aiden knew he wouldn't be able to protect his children from everything seen or unseen, but there were situations he could control, and escorting his daughters to the dance was one. But it still didn't solve the dilemma of his inability to dance.

"How many hours do we have to practice?"

Taryn turned, grinning from ear to ear. She held out her hand. "Probably thirty minutes a day, twice a week. I think it's best if we practice when the girls aren't around. We don't want them to know Daddy needs lessons. Let's start now. We'll begin slowly, until you feel comfortable moving your feet."

Aiden clasped Taryn's right hand while at the same time curving his right arm around her waist. He smiled. Her offering to teach him to dance wasn't a bad idea because he now had an excuse to hold her close. "I hope you don't expect me to turn into a John Travolta or Patrick Swayze."

Tilting her chin, Taryn met his eyes. "No. I'm thinking more along the lines of Bruno Mars."

"Oh, hell no, Taryn. There's no way I'm going to learn to dance like Bruno Mars." He still remembered Mars's electrifying performance during his first Super Bowl halftime show. "He's a natural showman."

"And you're a natural athlete, Aiden. Didn't you tell me that you were a competitive swimmer?"

"Yes, but—"

"No buts," she interrupted. "Look at the number of athletes who've won the *Dancing with the Stars* mirror ball."

"I never watch the show."

"Well you should, because some of the celebrities start out with two left feet before they learn ballroom dancing. I'm not a professional dancer, but I can teach you some of the more popular moves. Jessica told me they always do the Electric Slide, and 'Uptown Funk' always brings down the house."

Aiden's eyes moved slowly over Taryn's face. How did he expect to concentrate on learning to dance when his body was reminding him of how long it had been since he'd had a woman in his arms? "Are you going to grade my progress?"

Taryn stared up at him through her lashes. "Do you want me to?"

"Yes."

She took a step closer. "Close your eyes and concentrate on the music."

Aiden closed his eyes. In that instant his senses of

smell, touch and hearing were sharpened. "I like this song."

"Do you recognize the singer?"

"Yes. It's John Mayer."

"Do you like him?"

"Yes," Aiden confirmed.

"He's good to dance to because most of his songs are ballads. I have an extensive playlist on my smartphone and I'll go through it and select the ones we can dance to. I'll also ask Jessica to give me a list of the more popular tunes they've played over the years." Aiden went completely still when Taryn's breasts grazed his chest. "You're going to have to relax, Aiden."

"I'm trying," he said between clenched teeth. How did Taryn expect him to relax when their bodies were touching from knees to chest? Aiden forced himself to think about anything but the soft crush of firm breasts and the delicate fragrance of Taryn's perfume wafting in his nostrils.

"That's better," Taryn crooned. "Now bend your knees slightly and slowly move your hips in time with the music."

Aiden concentrated on the lyrics of "Slow Dancing in a Burning Room." That's exactly what he and Taryn were doing. Slow dancing, and his body had become the burning room. He was on fire, but he was grateful there was no repeat of the time when he'd walked into Taryn's bedroom to see her breasts in the sheer top that left little to his imagination.

"I don't know why you don't dance, because you do have rhythm."

"I didn't do much hanging out as a teenager because I was hitting the books and the pool."

"How about football games?"

Aiden opened his eyes. "I went to a few home games. Remember, I was on the swim team and we had to travel around the state to compete."

"Had you ever considered trying out for a higher-level team?"

"Nah. I was good, but not good enough for a world-class team."

"Why are you so modest?"

"It's not modesty, Taryn. I'm a very strong swimmer, but I'm no Michael Phelps."

"Do your kids swim?"

"Yes. I taught them as toddlers. What about you?"

"I was a little older when I learned. I was six when my parents sent me to sleepaway camp for the first time. The camp was in New Hampshire, and instead of a pool, we had to swim in a lake. I thought I'd never get warm. The cabins weren't heated, so we slept in sleeping bags at night. Even though it was hot during the daytime hours, the lake never warmed up. I came home with a swimmer's badge and it hung on a bulletin board in my room until I left for college."

"Do you have a swimsuit with you?"

Taryn leaned back to look at him. "No. Why?"

"There's a sports club in a town not far from here that offers daily passes to use their facilities to those who don't have a membership. I usually take the girls there several times a year so they can keep up their skills."

"I can usually do a couple of laps, but then I'm done."

"It takes a while before you're able to increase your endurance to do more. I don't work Sundays, so if you want, we can go swimming and just hang out." His arm tightened around Taryn's waist, causing her to stiffen before she went pliant in his embrace. Aiden felt the rapid beating of her heart against his chest.

"Have you forgotten that the Super Bowl is next Sunday?" Her query came out in a breathless whisper.

"No. I'm usually at the Den to put the meat in the smoker the night before and then go in around six Sunday morning to check on it. After that, I make the sides."

"If you plan to make guacamole, then don't throw away the seeds. I want to show Allison and Livia what to do to turn them into a plant."

"How many seeds do you want? Because I have one ripening in a bag on the countertop."

"Two more. Just wrap them in moistened paper towels and put them in a plastic bag to keep them from drying out."

"Yes, ma'am."

"Why do you keep calling me ma'am?"

"Have you forgotten that you're in the South where folks like us say, 'yes, ma'am' and 'no, sir?'"

"I suppose it's something I'll just have to get used to." Taryn dropped her arm. "That's enough practicing for today. You did very well for your first lesson. I came down here with the intent of taking a nap, but I think I'm going to take a walk instead."

Aiden released Taryn, feeling the separation immediately. He had enjoyed their physical contact. There was something about Taryn, other than her outward beauty that had him enthralled with her. She had taken charge when Livia demanded to wear her fairy outfit. He had watched her intently when she sat between the girls at Ruthie's, giving each equal attention. Aiden knew she was good for his children, and he knew having her around would make him a better father.

There were times when he realized he was too lenient with his daughters because he felt guilty and partially to blame that they were being raised without a mother. Even when Denise had known he wouldn't come home every night like most husbands, and she'd agreed to marry him. Six months into their marriage, she had begun complaining about everything. She hadn't liked the apartment he'd rented, so he contacted a real estate agent to purchase a house. The day they moved into their new home Denise was happier than he had ever seen her. She was like a little girl with a new dollhouse she couldn't wait to decorate. When she couldn't decide what type of fabric or style of furniture she wanted, he stepped in and hired a professional decorator.

They'd decided to wait a year before adding to their family, but when it didn't happen, Denise blamed his absences for preventing her from becoming pregnant. It reached the point where Aiden dreaded coming home to a wife who moaned about everything. Instead of coming back to Wickham Falls, he found himself spending more time in San Diego.

The separation made him aware that Denise had been too young and much too immature for marriage. He'd been a twenty-five-year-old navy SEAL and Denise, a nineteen-year-old shampoo girl in a local salon. And he'd married her for the wrong reason: he'd wanted to give her respectability.

They had just celebrated their fourth wedding anniversary when they had Allison, and eleven months later, Livia was born and it was as if a switch had gone off in his wife's head and she turned into someone he did not know or recognize. Any and everything he said or did would set her off where she'd scream and throw objects at him. Her erratic behavior had him questioning her ability to care for their children, and he arranged for his mother to come up and take her grandchildren to Florida for several weeks when he received orders to accompany other private military contractors to a country in the Middle East. The mission was to rescue an American businessman held for ransom by terrorists who wanted the United States to release one of their leaders.

When he returned, Aiden discovered Denise had left his children at his sister's with a note that she was moving to Austin, Texas. She gave him the address where he could send the divorce papers. He was stunned when she said she was willing to relinquish all parental rights and responsibility for their children. It took less than a month to have a lawyer draw up the documents for divorce and Denise kept her word when she signed the papers and mailed them back to the attorney's office. Six months later, the divorce was finalized and Aiden found himself a single father with a two- and three-year-old.

When Taryn asked if he would marry again, he'd been truthful when he told her maybe he would when the girls were older. He liked women, enjoyed their company and physical contact. And he would be able to offer a woman the stability he hadn't been able to give Denise, and that was something he would regret for the rest of his life.

He smiled at Taryn as she waved to him and headed for the door. Aiden debated whether to take a nap or cook enough for the following day's lunch and dinner; he decided on the latter. He'd worked late Saturday night and hadn't gotten home until after one. Then he'd had to get up at seven to drive up to Charleston to be at the airport. He'd planned to roast the chicken for dinner and use the leftovers to make soup and a Cobb salad for Monday's lunch. He still hadn't decided what to prepare for the following day's dinner. Although he maintained a fully stocked refrigerator/freezer, Aiden had made it known to Taryn that she didn't have to cook for him or his daughters. If she didn't want to eat what he'd prepared, she had the option of cooking for herself.

Livia and Allison leaving their clothes on the floor was a sore spot with him but so far, he hadn't been able to get them to stop, short of raising his voice. And he'd done that enough when living with their mother and vowed he would not repeat it with his children.

Taryn mentioning his hosting of the Super Bowl party had him thinking about whether or not to diversify the menu he offered his family and friends. Once she returned from her walk, he would solicit her input.

Chapter Eight

Taryn was standing at the entrance to the classroom when Livia and Allison arrived. She'd informed them the night before that classes began promptly at nine o'clock and she expected them to have eaten breakfast, bathed, dressed and be ready to learn. Both sported damp hair from a shower and were dressed in jeans, long-sleeved T-shirts and sneakers.

"Good morning, Allison, Livia. How are you?"

"Good," they chorused, smiling.

"Before we go in, I'd like to know if your bedrooms are neat and clean." Her query was met with Allison lifting her shoulders and Livia's blank expression. "I'm asking because when you saw your classroom yesterday, you may have noticed that everything is in its own place. There were no puzzle pieces on the floor or books left out. It should be the same with your bedrooms.

Now, we're going upstairs to inspect your rooms and if you left anything out, then you have to put it away." She smiled. "Let's go."

Taryn wasn't surprised when she saw dresser drawers open with articles of clothing spilling out and on the floor. She ignored the unmade bed because it wasn't crucial they learn to make a bed when compared to clean and dirty clothes strewn around the room.

"Allison, I want you to separate the clean clothes from the soiled ones. Put the dirty clothes in the bathroom hamper and then come back and fold the clean ones and put them away." She reached for Livia's hand. "You're going to do the same in your bedroom."

Livia's face fell. "But we're going to be late for school."

"I know, and I'll have to mark you late. And I know you don't want to be late for a movie party on Friday."

She must have gotten through to Livia, as she raced through the connecting bath and into her bedroom. Meanwhile, Taryn quickly made up the twin bed, fluffing up the pillows and placing a worn gray stuffed dog on the window seat. She went into Allison's room and made her bed, too. After the girls got into a habit of putting away their clothes, Taryn would teach them how to make their beds. Tidiness was essential for them if or when they would have to share a dorm room with another student.

As a freshman at Howard, she had shared a dorm with a girl who would invariably bring food back to the room and leave leftovers under her bed. Taryn lost her temper when the room became infested with insects and other vermin. Her sophomore year fared a little better when she didn't have to deal with decaying food but dirty clothes. Whenever her roommate stepped out of something it remained there.

By her junior year, Taryn had had enough and moved into off-campus housing. Taryn felt as if she had been redeemed when Jessica transferred from a college in Pittsburgh to Washington, DC, to become her roommate. Jessica was even more anal than she was when it came to putting everything in its place. As education majors, they bonded quickly, and within months, regarded each other as sisters from another mister.

"Very nice," she said, complimenting Allison. "This is how your room should look every morning before you come down to the classroom. Let's see how Livia is doing." They walked into Livia's bedroom and found nothing on the carpet. "Wow! How nice everything looks. I'm so proud of you girls."

Taryn tested and evaluated each girl and discovered they were equally proficient in writing their names, recognizing numbers one through ten and many letters in the alphabet. She then directed them to the reading corner for a read-aloud.

Taryn sat on a beanbag chair, while Allison and Livia shared another bag. "Today, I'm going to read a story about a pig and spider."

Livia scrunched up her tiny nose. "I don't like spiders."

Taryn gave her a reassuring smile. "I think you're going to like this spider. Her name is Charlotte."

"What's the pig's name?" Allison asked.

"Wilbur." The girls laughed hysterically.

"Wilbur is a funny name for a pig," Livia said.

"It is," Taryn said in agreement. She read the first

two chapters, pausing to show them the beautiful illustrations. She closed the book. "We'll continue this tomorrow because it's time for lunch."

Allison pushed out her lips. "Can you read more after lunch?"

Taryn knew they would like E. B. White's *Charlotte's Web*. The book was one of her personal favorites, along with *Madeline*, *The Snowy Day* and the *Frog and Toad* series. "After lunch you're going to take a short nap and after you get up, we're going outside to play kickball."

"What are we going to do after kickball?" Allison asked again.

"You'll have a snack."

"After the snack?" Livia questioned.

"We're either going to play a board game or put a puzzle together." Taryn averted her head so they wouldn't see her smile. Although Aiden's daughters were full of questions, they hadn't rejected her suggestion they take a nap. "Who's going to help me set the table so we can eat?"

"Me!"

"Me, too!"

Taryn led them into the kitchen, opening the drawer with serving pieces. "We need three forks and three spoons."

Allison peered in the drawer. "Do you want big forks or little forks, Miss Taryn?"

"We need one big fork, two little ones and the same with the spoons. I'm going to get some napkins and show you how to put them on the table."

Twenty minutes later, they sat around the table in the classroom and said grace before enjoying a lunch of delicious homemade chicken soup, Cobb salad, a fruit cup of green grapes and sliced strawberries, and chilled milk. Taryn elicited their help clearing the table and loading the dishwasher, hoping it would carry over to them volunteering to perform the task for other meals.

After pulling down the woven blinds, Taryn set out two cots with pillows and extinguished all the lights. Livia and Allison removed their shoes, lay on the cots and she covered both with lightweight blankets.

Taryn put on a disc featuring music for relaxation, and settled down on the beanbag with a paperback novel. She felt rather than saw movement and glanced up to see Aiden peer through the partially closed doors. After breakfast, he'd announced he was going out and would be back later that afternoon. Pushing off the chair, she approached him, pulling him out of earshot of the napping children. Stubble covered his head and it was obvious he'd gotten a haircut.

Aiden curved an arm around Taryn's waist. "How's it going?"

"Everything's great. Right now they're napping." Taryn revealed to him that she had gotten Livia and Allison to pick up their clothes, taught them to set and clear the table and load dishes into the dishwasher.

He shook his head in amazement. "You're definitely a miracle worker."

Taryn flashed a demure smile. "Not quite. It's just that I have a lot of experience working with children."

Aiden wanted to tell Taryn that she was being overly modest. She'd gotten his children to do what she wanted in one day, something he hadn't been able to accomplish after telling them to do something over and over until he finally gave up.

"I'm going make dinner before leaving for work. Is there something you'd like to eat?"

"I've been craving spaghetti with marinara sauce."

"No meatballs?"

Taryn pulled her lip between her teeth. "No. Not unless you want to make them for the girls?"

"What if I grill some shrimp, meatballs and sausage and you can select whatever you want?"

"That sounds good."

Aiden stared at Taryn from under lowered lids, marveling that she could look so sexy without a hint of makeup. "When's the next dance lesson?" He was anxious to hold her under the guise that she had become his dance instructor.

"Tonight."

"But I won't be home until after eleven."

"Don't worry about that. I'll be in the basement watching television. I'm going back before they wake up."

Aiden blew out his breath as he watched Taryn walk, unable to pull his eyes away from the fluid sway of her hips. There were times when he cursed her for being so damned sexy, but that wasn't her problem; it was his. How, he mused, was he going to survive the next eleven months with Taryn living under his roof and not blurt out that she turned him on in a way no other woman had?

He had been able to control his libido when dancing together, yet his body had betrayed him when he woke earlier that morning with an extremely hard erection. His first instinct was to go into the bathroom, stand under the shower and relieve himself—something he hadn't done since adolescence, but instead he waited for the pleasurable throbbing to ebb. Aiden hadn't slept with so many women that they had become a trail of forgotten names and faces, because his father had preached to him that women were not there to be used, but respected.

When he enlisted in the navy, he hadn't had a high school sweetheart or lover waiting for his return. He'd left Wickham Falls unencumbered and without any entanglements. And he'd never slept with a woman and not used protection. At that time he hadn't been ready to become a father when he hadn't fulfilled his dream of becoming special ops.

His cell phone chimed a familiar ringtone. Aiden retrieved the phone from the pocket of his jeans. It was his uncle. "What's up, Jonah?"

"Can you switch your shift with Tommy?"

"When?"

"Tonight. He wants to come in tonight because he has a doctor's appointment tomorrow morning."

Aiden's expression stilled and grew serious. "Is he all right?"

"He says he is. He told me when I first hired him that he'd been diagnosed with a heart murmur. He was seeing a cardiologist when he lived in Michigan, and now he has to follow up with one up in Charleston."

"Damn, Uncle, why didn't he say anything to me?"

"Don't get your nose out of joint, Aiden. Tommy probably sees you as his big brother, while I'm more like a father to him."

Aiden did not want to believe he worked side by side with his cousin and not once had he opened up about his medical condition. "Do you think you should cut back his hours?" he asked Jonah.

"I've been thinking about it. But I don't want him to think we're mollycoddling him because of his heart."

"We wouldn't be mollycoddling him, Jonah. He just can't continue working twelve-hour days, six days a week. We can get Luke to take over some of his hours."

"Maybe it's time we have a staff meeting and redefine everyone's responsibilities. You, Luke and Fletcher have kids, and that means you guys will get first preference when it comes to the hours which work best for you. I will definitely defer to you because you're the single father."

Aiden wanted to remind Jonah that although he was a single father, he'd hired a professional who was not only trustworthy but reliable to look after his children. "We'll talk about it once you schedule the meeting. And tell Tommy I don't mind coming in tomorrow morning."

"I'll let him know. And thanks for being flexible."

Aiden rolled his eyes upward. "Come on, Jonah. Don't go and get wussy on me."

"Bye, Aiden."

Jonah didn't give him a chance to respond by ending the call. Now that his shift had changed, he would spend the night with Taryn and his children.

This is what a family looks like when sharing dinner. He could not recall the last time he had sat down and shared the evening meal with Denise and their children. She had taken her meals on the porch regardless of the weather, claiming it was there that she felt free.

It had only taken a few days for Taryn to bring stability and organization to his household; when they sat down at the table, his daughters quickly reminded him they couldn't eat until someone said grace. He had sheepishly lowered his head and listened with pride as Allison gave thanks for the food on the table, the farmers who grew it and for the hands that prepared it. He'd met Taryn's eyes and pantomimed his thanks.

Touching his napkin to the corners of his mouth, he smiled at Allison. "I've decided to take you girls to the Father/Daughter Dance."

Livia gasped and then blurted out, "Really, Daddy?"

"You're not joking?" Allison asked, her face flushed with high color.

Aiden smiled. "No, I'm not kidding."

Allison squirmed in excitement. "We have to wear costumes."

"We have to go to the party store to buy costumes," Livia said quickly.

Aiden met Taryn's direct stare. She'd mentioned making costumes but had not wanted to tell them in advance. "Don't worry about costumes."

"I'll make them for you," Taryn stated. "This year's theme is a magical forest with fairies, elves, leprechauns and gnomes. Livia, I know you want to be a fairy. Allison, you have to let me know what you want to be."

Allison's dark eyes brightened. "I want to be an elf with pointed ears and shoes."

Taryn nodded. "Saturday morning, we'll go into town to the fabric store and pick up the materials we'll need to make the costumes."

"Am I going to have a costume for my birthday party?" Livia asked.

Aiden smiled at his youngest daughter. "I was thinking of doing something very special for your birthday."

"What is it, Daddy?"

"I'm not sure, because I'm still thinking about it, but I'm certain you're going to be surprised."

Livia's mouth formed a perfect O. "Does Miss Taryn know the surprise?"

"No. But once I finalize it, I'll talk to her about it."

Allison swirled spaghetti around her fork. "Will Miss Taryn be at the surprise?"

"Why?" Aiden asked.

"Because I want her there," Allison said.

Livia bobbed her head. "I want her there, too."

Aiden knew his daughters had put him and Taryn on the spot. "You're going to have to wait until I talk to Miss Taryn about the surprise before I can give you an answer. Maybe she will have something else planned for that day." His response seemed to satisfy the girls, and they concentrated on eating the food on their plates.

Staring over the rim of her wineglass, Taryn saw something in Aiden's eyes she hadn't noticed before. She wasn't certain whether it was curiosity or an emotion that went deeper than his appreciation for his daughters' progress over the past week.

They'd just finished a dance lesson and to celebrate Aiden learning all of the steps to the Electric Slide, he'd suggested they uncork a bottle of cabernet sauvignon. She touched her glass to his. "Congratulations! You just earned your first A."

Smiling, lines fanning out around his luminous eyes, Aiden hoisted his glass. "Here's to the best teacher in and out of the classroom."

"Only because your girls are little geniuses." Allison and Livia were now able to trace the letters in their first and last names, count to twenty and recognize numbers out of sequence. They loved reading stories aloud and playing outdoors, weather permitting. Once they realized they were going to see the movie based on the book Taryn had read to them, it had taken a full five minutes before she was able to get them to calm down enough to watch *Charlotte's Web*. She'd delayed starting the movie so she could make popcorn, which sent her approval rating with her students off the chart.

"And I'm certain my little geniuses are bending their cousins' ears about their fabulous teacher and amazing classroom."

Taryn took a sip of wine. "Do they come here?"

Aiden shook his head. "Hardly ever. My sister complains that her house is too small, but that doesn't stop her from inviting Livia and Allie for sleepovers."

Unfolding her legs tucked under her body, Taryn leaned over and placed the wineglass on a side table. She exhaled an audible breath. "I've got a cramp in my leg." Shifting on the loveseat, Aiden anchored his hands under her thighs and rested her legs over his knees. She closed her eyes as he massaged her bare feet and legs. "Oo-ooo. That feels good." His strong fingers sent shivers of awareness over her body, reminding her how long it had been since a man had caressed her bare skin.

Lifting her leg, Aiden bent over and planted a kiss on her instep. "Do you always wear polish on your toes?"

Warming sensations eddied through her when his mouth touched her foot. The kiss may have been innocent enough, but for Taryn it was as sensual as if he'd kissed her mouth. It took several seconds before she was able to form a reply as she wiggled the vermilion-colored digits. "Yes. I change color with the seasons.

Red for winter, pink for spring, white for summer and orange for fall. I promised Allison and Livia that I would take them with me when I go for a mani/pedi."

"I hope you know what you're doing because they'll want it all the time."

Taryn tried to make out Aiden's features in the diffused light. He'd dimmed the recessed lights, creating an atmosphere that reminded her of a nightclub. "That's all right. They're real girlie-girls." She moaned softly when he increased the pressure of his thumb on her calf.

"Did I hurt you?"

"No." The single word was barely a whisper. "I think it's time I head upstairs and go to bed. Don't forget you have…" Whatever she attempted to say was preempted when Aiden stood, bringing her up with him. "What are you doing?"

His nose brushed against her cheek. "Taking you to bed."

Her arms went around his neck to keep her balance. "I can walk by myself."

"Can you let me play superhero just this once?"

Taryn couldn't believe Aiden held her as effortlessly as he would a small child. She felt his breath on her forehead and the strong steady beating of his heart against the side of her breast. He'd held her hand, danced with her, but his holding her to his chest sent ripples of desire racing through her body like a fuse attached to a stick of dynamite.

She'd spent a little more than a week attempting to ignore the man who was her boss; and she'd refused to acknowledge that she was more attracted to him than she was willing to admit.

Taryn knew there was something special about

Aiden that went beyond his dedication to his family and children, and the more time she spent with him, the harder it was for her to differentiate from Aiden the devoted father and the soft-spoken, respectful man who, despite his lustful glances, had not attempted to come on to her. Although he looked nothing like the men with whom she found herself attracted to in the past, she knew he was someone she could seriously consider becoming more than a good friend. The major obstacle was she was his children's teacher and even more importantly, she was living under his roof.

Taryn nodded and buried her face against the column of his strong neck. "Okay, Batman."

Aiden shifted Taryn, marveling that she felt so light in his arms as he walked across the basement and climbed the staircase to the first floor. "Tomorrow, you'll be able to sleep in late."

Taryn rested her head on his shoulder. "It's already tomorrow."

"You're right about that."

It was Super Bowl Sunday and more than twelve hours from now his home would be filled with family and friends. Once he had revealed what he intended to offer to his guests, Taryn had suggested he diversify the menu to include a charcuterie-and-cheese platter. She had also volunteered to buy the ingredients and create the dish. Aiden had given her the go-ahead, because he was curious to see what she would come up with. Taryn was sharing his house, and beginning tomorrow they would cook together, hoping it would become the first of many more encounters.

Just knowing she was in the house made it feel like

a real home for the first time in years. Not only was she good for his daughters, but also for him.

"I don't want you to get out of bed *today* before nine."

"Is that an order?"

He smiled. "It's a direct order."

"Do you miss the military?"

Taryn had asked Aiden a question he had asked himself over and over since his honorable discharge and the answer was always ambivalence. "Yes and no." He turned down the hallway leading to Taryn's bedroom and entered the suite. She'd left on the bedside lamp.

"Why yes?"

"From the moment I was sworn in, it was as if I'd received a transfusion of all things military. It was in my blood. The more rigorous the training, the better, and I was always looking for the next challenge. It never crossed my mind to drop out of BUD/S when my buddies were. For me, once in, then all in. My class started out with almost two hundred and in the end, only thirty-four graduated." Aiden placed Taryn on the bed, and he sat on the side of the mattress, sandwiching his hands between his knees.

Taryn rested a hand on his back. "And why don't you miss it?"

Aiden sucked in a lungful of air, held it for several seconds before exhaling. Something wouldn't allow him to lie to Taryn. He trusted her with his children, and that meant he had to trust her enough to confide the details of his marriage. "If my ex hadn't walked out on our children and if my uncle was still alive, I would still be working as a private contractor."

Taryn sat up, swung her legs over the side of the bed and held his hand. "Tell me about it." Her voice was soft, coaxing, the same tone she used when attempting to get Livia and Allison to do something she wanted.

Aiden gently squeezed her fingers. It was as if the floodgates had been opened and he told Taryn everything. His combat missions as a SEAL and his subsequent career as a military contractor. He also revealed the circumstances surrounding his first encounter with Denise Wilkinson when he saw her sitting in her car in a parking lot crying inconsolably; she'd been fired from her housekeeping job at a motel because the owner suspected she had been smoking marijuana. Her boss didn't believe her explanation when she said she'd been with her brother who smoked weed in the house every day.

"I gave her some money and told her everything would work out."

"Did it?"

"Yes. She found a job at a salon as a shampoo girl. After she got her first paycheck she came to my mom's house and returned the money I'd given her."

"How old was she?"

"Denise had just turned nineteen. I took her out a couple of times before I had to go back to San Diego. When I came home again, we reconnected and it wasn't until we slept together that I discovered she was a virgin."

"Did you get her pregnant?"

"No."

"But, you did the right thing and married her."

He turned and stared at Taryn's delicate profile. "How did you know?"

"Because you're a good guy."

"I wasn't trying to be a good guy. I just didn't want to take advantage of her. Denise's family doesn't have the best reputation around these parts. Her mother and father were arrested for domestic battery, while her deadbeat brothers wouldn't be able to keep their asses out of jail or prison even if they won the Powerball. One is serving hard time for manslaughter, and a few others have rap sheets for robbery, drugs and assault. Denise is the only Wilkinson who wanted better for herself."

Aiden paused and carefully chose his words before revealing further details of his marriage that he'd never told anyone—and that included his mother. He felt Taryn tense when he bared his soul about coming home after clandestine missions to find his wife passed out in bed and their children crying inconsolably in their cribs. "My uncle, who'd helped Jonah run the Den, passed away, and that's when I decided not to renew my contract with the security company and stepped in to assist Jonah. It was the first time in almost fifteen years that I wouldn't have to grab my gear and ship out. Living with Denise full-time had become a nightmare. Our arguments escalated into shouting matches that affected our daughters because they'd start crying and wouldn't stop. I'd picked them up and walk the floor until they fell asleep. Even when I want to raise my voice at my girls, I refuse to do it because I'm afraid it will elicit flashbacks of what went on between me and their mother."

"Do you have proof they remember the arguments between you and their mother?"

"Livia doesn't, but every once in a while Allie will mention something about Denise. She was three when Denise told her she was going away and never coming back because she didn't love her and her daddy."

A gasp escaped Taryn. "What a horribly cruel thing to tell a child."

"There were times when Denise could be soft and loving and other times when she was incredibly cruel. Several months before she decided to leave she was diagnosed as bipolar, and if she was off her meds, then the ugly side of her personality surfaced. People were calling her tramp because they claimed she'd slept with other men when I was away but I dismissed it as gossip. Folks were always looking for a reason to lump her into the same category as the other members of her family."

"Do you still love her?"

Aiden stared ahead, complete surprise freezing his features. He had expected Taryn to ask if he missed Denise, not if he still loved her. "No, because she wouldn't let me love her," he said after a swollen silence. "She complained when I went away for weeks or months at a time, and she complained when I was home for extended periods of time because she claimed she felt smothered. I may no longer love her, but I definitely don't hate her. She gave me two precious children, and for that I'll always be grateful."

Taryn untangled their fingers, put her arm around his waist and laid her head on his shoulder. "They are precious."

He smiled. "You have to know they adore you. Whenever we're together it's always Miss Taryn said this and Miss Taryn said we shouldn't do that."

"That's because kids in lower grades are fascinated with their teachers."

Aiden rested his chin on the top of Taryn's head. He wondered how many fathers of her students had become fascinated with her. "Now you know the whole sordid details of my turbulent marriage."

"There's no need to beat up on yourself, Aiden. If you hadn't married Denise, then you wouldn't have had Allison and Livia. You risked your life serving our country; you tried to be a good husband and are an incredible father. At least give yourself credit for all that."

Wrapping both arms around Taryn, Aiden buried his face in her hair. She had no idea how good she was to and for him. Her being there had offered him a sense of normalcy for the first time in years. He woke looking forward to seeing her and his children. And when he came home, even if they were in bed, it felt as if invisible arms were welcoming him in.

Taryn being there represented everything he'd hoped for when he married Denise: a cohesive family unit with father, mother and children. However, the distinct difference was she wasn't the mother of his children, and it wasn't for the first time he wondered what if he'd met and married her first and she'd had his children.

He kissed her hair. "It's time I leave, so you can get some sleep."

Easing back, Taryn smiled up at him. "Good night."

Aiden stared at her parted lips, longing to taste them. Common sense swept over him at the last possible moment before he lowered his head and kissed her forehead. "Good night."

He stood and walked out of the suite, his reaction to Taryn in a whirlwind of confusion. Nothing in her attitude indicated she wanted anything from him beyond friendship, and he knew he had to control his emotions or he would risk losing her.

Chapter Nine

"Look who's here."

Taryn's head popped up when Aiden walked into the kitchen with her friends. She'd spent the last forty-five minutes creating a charcuterie-and-cheese platter. When she woke earlier that morning, she discovered she had the house to herself. Aiden had left to go to the Den to smoke meat and Livia and Allison were still at their Aunt Esther's house. She used the time to search through the well-stocked pantry and refrigerator to prepare several items to add to the Super Bowl menu: a medley of seasonal fruit and two sour cream pound cakes.

A wide smile spread over her features. Wiping her hands on a towel, she came over to greet Jessica and Sawyer. The night before Aiden told her that he had invited them to join his family for their annual Super

Bowl get-together. Jessica wore a Pittsburgh Steelers sweatshirt with black jeans and yellow running shoes, while her husband sported a New York Giants sweatshirt.

Residents wearing sweatshirts or T-shirts with college or football team logos on Super Bowl Sunday had become a longtime favored tradition in The Falls. Taryn had gone through her collection of sports paraphernalia and found several with Howard University and New York professional teams.

She hugged Jessica and then Sawyer. Taryn cut her eyes at him. "What's with a West Virginia homey wearing my team's shirt?" Taryn planned to put on her New York Giants T-shirt before she joined the others in the basement.

The intense Caribbean winter sun had lightened Sawyer's dark wavy hair with streaks of red and darkened his face to highlight a pair of large sapphire-blue eyes. Sawyer did not know that if Taryn hadn't convinced Jessica not to end her engagement to him, her friend had talked about not marrying him. Jessica felt as if her fiancé had blindsided her when he'd wanted to surprise her with the news that he'd accepted a position as the head of the school district's technology department.

"Have you forgotten I still have a New York City address, Miss New-to-Wickham-Falls," Sawyer teased.

"There's nothing wrong with Wickham Falls," Taryn said in defense of her new hometown.

"Hear, hear!" intoned Aiden, as he cradled a carton of whiskey against his sweatshirt stamped with an army/navy football matchup. "Sawyer and Jessica brought us a case of Jack Daniels."

Taryn wanted to tell Aiden that the Middletons had brought *him* a case of Jack Daniels because she tended not to drink hard liquor. "Thank you very much!" she drawled in her best Elvis Presley imitation.

Smiling, Aiden motioned with his head. "You guys head on downstairs. I just want to warn you that my brother-in-law, Fletcher, is tending bar, and he can be rather heavy-handed with the libations."

Jessica patted her husband's shoulder. "Go on down without me. I'm going to stay and help Taryn."

Sawyer kissed his wife's forehead. "No problem, babe."

Aiden winked at Taryn. "Call me if you need my help with anything."

She smiled and nodded. "I will."

Jessica waited for the two men to leave the kitchen before she turned her attention to Taryn. "What's going on with you and Aiden?"

Taryn's hands halted arranging tiny parmesan short-breads and herbed pita crisps on the large platter with an assortment of cheeses and thinly sliced cured meats. "What are you talking about?"

Jessica moved closer. "Do you need glasses?"

A frown found its way between her eyes. "What on earth are you talking about?"

"Aiden has the hots for you," Jessica whispered.

"You're bugging."

"Am I really, my friend? You're living in the same house with a man whose face is as easy to read as a large print book. His eyes don't lie whenever he looks at you. There's lust in them there blue-green orbs. Do you know what they're saying?"

"No. Please enlighten me."

"He sees you as a golden-brown biscuit he'd like to sop up with some syrup."

Throwing back her head, Taryn laughed loudly. "You *are* bugging. There's nothing going on between me and Aiden, because I don't want anything to happen."

"Why not?"

"If I got involved with him, it would seriously affect my relationship with his kids."

"How so?"

"They relate to me as their teacher and not as a stepmother."

Jessica crossed her arms under her breasts and rested a hip against the countertop. "You don't find yourself attracted to Aiden?"

Taryn eyelids fluttered wildly. Jessica was asking a question she'd asked herself over and over since moving to Wickham Falls. "That's not an easy question to answer because he's my boss."

"You wouldn't be the first employee to get involved with her boss."

"I know that, but there are too many roadblocks that won't allow me to think of him romantically. I'm not going to sleep with Aiden and then have him sneak out of my bed or me out of his before his daughters discover us together."

A hint of a smile lifted the corners of Jessica's mouth. "So you would consider sleeping with him?"

"Duh! He is a man and it's been a while since I've had one scratch my itch."

Jessica clapped a hand over her mouth as tears of laughter filled her eyes. "Where do you come up with these sayings? I keep saying you could've had a career in stand-up."

"Well it's true. The itch went away after I broke up with James, but since I've been around Aiden, it has come back with a vengeance." She told Jessica about her and Aiden drinking wine before they wound up on the bed in her bedroom. "It felt so natural for us to be together that I wondered what would've happened if I'd asked him to stay."

It had taken Taryn Herculean strength not to beg Aiden to make love to her. He was a constant reminder of what she'd had and lost: male companionship. She'd dated men she didn't sleep with and a few she had. And it wasn't so much about sex as it was about going places and doing things together. That's what she'd liked about James. They enjoyed attending sporting events, working out at a local sports club, dining alfresco during the warmer weather and sleeping in late on Sundays before going out for brunch and returning home to read the newspaper or binge-watch their favorite shows.

"Where were his girls?"

"They were at their aunt's house for a sleepover."

"Girl, please! It was the perfect opportunity to get him to scratch your itch."

"The next…" Her words trailed off when Aiden returned to the kitchen. "I'm finished with the platter," she said smoothly.

Aiden approached Taryn and rested his hand at the small of her back. He stared at the large platter of cheese, meat, nuts, a variety of dried and candied fruit, and an assortment of crackers. "It's the perfect subject for a still life painting."

She smiled up at him. "That's because I minored in art." Her upcoming lesson plans included several art projects for her eager students. They were like sponges soaking up everything they were exposed to. "I'm finished with it, so you can take it down. As soon as I change my smock, Jessica and I will join everyone."

"Folks have begun chowing down, so I wouldn't linger too long," Aiden warned.

"Now tell me I was wrong about him lusting after you?" Jessica asked after Aiden disappeared from earshot. "Even when he touched you, I could see it was proprietary."

Taryn wanted to tell Jessica to stop planning her love life. She looped her arm through Jessica's. "I'm going to give you a quick peek at the classroom before I change. Meanwhile, I want you answer something for me."

Jessica stared up at her with wide dark eyes. "What is it?"

"What's up with you trying to match me up with Aiden?"

"I want you to be happy. You deserve it—"

"Don't say it," Taryn said, interrupting her.

"Don't you want to be happy?"

"I am happy, Jessica. I live in a wonderful home with my own private quarters. I teach two delightful little girls who truly make me glad I've chosen to be an educator. Aiden is generous and easygoing and that's enough for me."

"Does this mean you're not opposed to dating someone who isn't your boss?"

"What are you talking about?"

"Don't act obtuse, Taryn. You know exactly what I'm talking about. The district just hired several new teachers and there's one I believe would be perfect for you."

Taryn shook her head. "No, no and no! I'm not interested nor do I have the time to date anyone." She stopped at the doors leading into the classroom. "I know you're trying to return the favor of me knocking some sense into that hard head of yours when you wanted to end your engagement to Sawyer. This is not about one hand washing the other, my friend."

"I know that," Jessica argued softly. "You don't realize when I transferred to Howard and roomed with you that you became my lifeline and got me to see what true friendship was all about. When I told you about my fiancé choosing to believe his frat brother's excuse that sex with my roommate was consensual when I knew it was rape devastated me. And to take the rag off the bush, he joined the others on campus when they bullied me for outing their NFL hopeful. You listened to me moan about his traitorous ass, dried my tears whenever I had a pity party and you made me laugh when you said you were willing to drive to Pittsburgh and administer some Big Apple justice when you threatened to hit him upside the head with a can of peas stuffed into a pair of pantyhose."

"Folks are lucky that I'm not violent or I'd go Ray Donovan and open the trunk of my car and knock the hell out of them with a baseball bat."

"You're a much stronger woman than I am, Taryn, because I don't think I'd be able to go to work and look at the tramp that slept with my man in *my* bed and not lose it."

"That's why every morning before walking into the school building I said the Serenity Prayer. It's what kept me sane, focused and out of prison." Taryn waved a hand as if banishing the memory of Aisha's smirking face whenever their paths crossed. Flipping a wall switch and opening the doors to the converted sunroom and back porch, she walked into the classroom. "This is where I spend most of my day."

With wide eyes, Jessica entered the classroom. "You've really done it." There was no mistaking the awe in her voice. "This is the best model kindergarten classroom I've ever seen. All you have to do is take a photo of this when you interview for a position for the district and they'll hire you on the spot."

"That's too far in the future for me to think about. I have this year and possibly the next year before I return to the traditional classroom. Come see where I sleep and relax during my downtime." Less than a minute later, Taryn led Jessica to her sleeping quarters.

Jessica walked into the spacious bedroom suite and then peered into the bathroom. "This is better than suites in some of the best luxury hotels. Who decorated Aiden's house?"

Bending slightly, Taryn opened a drawer in the armoire and searched through a stack of T-shirts. "I don't know. It could've been Aiden's ex or a professional decorator."

"Does he ever talk about his ex-wife?"

"A little," she admitted.

Taryn didn't feel comfortable divulging what Aiden had revealed less than twenty-four hours ago. She knew it hadn't been easy for him to talk about a woman with whom he had fallen in love and had given him two children. She also detected pain in his voice when he admitted to accepting blame for his failed marriage because of his frequent absences. She wanted to remind Aiden that Denise had known he was active military when she agreed to marry him but held her tongue.

She'd grown up with girls who'd married men for

various reasons other than love, and Taryn wondered if Denise had agreed to become Aiden's wife not because she loved him but because she wanted to distance herself from her family. However, in the end, she left The Falls, isolating herself from her family members, her husband and her children.

Taryn exchanged her painter's smock for a long-sleeved T-shirt stamped with the New York Giants. "I got Aiden to agree to bring his daughters to the Father/ Daughter Dance."

Jessica clasped her hands together. "They're going to have a ball."

"I've told Livia and Allison that I'm going to make their costumes. Livia is going to be a sparkling green fairy to match her eyes."

"What about Allison?"

"She wants to be an elf."

"With your art background and sewing skills, I know they'll look incredible."

"Let's hope you're right. I think we should go down and join the others before Aiden sends out a search party."

Mouthwatering aromas wafting from chafing dishes lining serving tables met them when they stepped off the last stair leading into the basement. Two picnic tables covered with football-decorated tablecloths and benches with padded seat cushions positioned end to end were filled with adult Gibsons and their extended family. The younger crowd sat together in the area with the game tables. The television, tuned to an all-sports channel, was muted, while music spanning several decades played softly from wireless speakers.

Jessica leaned closer to Taryn. "I'm willing to bet

the second we leave Sawyer's going to bug me about finishing the basement after seeing this one."

"I thought you guys had decided on what you wanted," Taryn said, as they stood in line at the serving tables. Jessica revealed Sawyer had become obsessed with converting their unfinished basement into a space where they could entertain friends and family.

"We'll talk about that later," Jessica said sotto voce.

Taryn picked up two plates, one she filled with a tossed salad and the other with Buffalo wings, grilled steak fingers, baked beans and coleslaw. She found a seat cushion next to Aiden's sister. Taryn had met Esther for the first time when she'd come to pick up her nieces for a sleepover at her home.

The attractive dental hygienist with dirty blond hair and green eyes pointed to Taryn's plate. "Are you on a diet?"

"No." Fortunately, she never had to monitor her weight.

"Well, it looks like it from what's on your plate."

Taryn smiled. "This is only the first course. The next one will include what I need to go into a meat coma: ribs, brisket and pulled pork."

Esther flashed a wide grin. "There was a time when I was pregnant with my first daughter and I was craving pork like an addict needing his next fix. I had a big plate of ribs, pulled pork and fried pork belly and wound up sick as a dog. When I told Fletcher what I'd eaten, he said I'd come down with swine flu. That was the first and last time I ate that much pork in one sitting."

Taryn covered her mouth with her hand to keep the laughter bubbling up in her throat from escaping. She knew what Esther was talking about; she'd overdosed on the most delicious chitterlings she'd ever eaten and paid for overindulging the next day. It took years before she attempted to try them again.

"Hey, Taryn," Fletcher called out from behind the bar. "What can I get you to drink?"

"I'll have a cola." It was the first thing that had popped into her head.

"Can I put a little Jack in that cola?"

She shook her head. "No, thank you."

"Scared?" Fletcher teased.

"Stop badgering my girl," Aiden said before Taryn could answer.

"I thought I was your girl?" piped up Livia from the other side of room.

Aiden turned to smile at her. "You are. And so are Allie and Miss Taryn."

"She ain't no girl," Jonathan, Luke's eight-year-old son, called out. "She's only a lady."

"She's not only a lady," Allison said angrily. "She's also my teacher."

"She ain't no teacher," Jonathan shot back. "Miss Calhoun is a teacher."

Aiden knew it was time to end the debate or it would escalate into a full-blown argument with his daughters in the center of the fray. "Jonathan, Miss Taryn is a lady *and* a teacher."

Jonathan stuck out his tongue at Allison, who returned in kind. "See. I told you she was a teacher," she spat out.

It was apparent Lucas had seen enough when he walked over his son and whispered something in his ear. The little boy's face became pale and then a flush crept up from his neck to his hairline. "I'm sorry, Allie, for sticking my tongue out at you," Jonathan said, apologizing to his cousin.

Allison shot a quick glance at Aiden when he cleared his throat. The expression on his face spoke volumes: he was disappointed. "I'm sorry, too, Jonathan."

There came a collective sigh as if everyone had been holding their breaths. Aiden had witnessed enough petty arguments between his daughters and his nephews to last a lifetime. It was as if they couldn't get along with their boy cousins and constantly traded barbs with one another. This time, he'd been surprised that it was Allison who'd come back at Jonathan. She rarely engaged in a verbal confrontation unless provoked, while Livia was his defiant little firecracker who always had to have the last word.

Aiden lifted his eyebrows when he met Taryn's eyes, wondering if she had become a party to his daughters' sibling rivalry. He'd lost track of the number of times he'd preached to them that as sisters they were not to fight but protect each other. He'd had to put Livia in timeout whenever her quick temper and even quicker hands got the better of her. And Aiden knew if he did enroll them in public school, Livia would be the one to confront anyone who bullied her or her sister, but he wanted to wait for them to develop the coping skills necessary to diffuse a situation without resorting to fighting.

His mouth twitched with amusement when Taryn gave him a barely perceptible nod and mysterious smile. After he'd revealed the circumstances of his failed marriage, Aiden felt as if he'd unburdened himself to a therapist. The guilt he'd carried for far too long had vanished once he'd come to the realization that because he didn't work a nine-to-five, he did what he had to do to provide for his family.

Denise knew even before they'd become intimately involved that the military was his career choice. He'd given her the option of continuing to see him whenever he came home on leave or they could stop seeing each other. She said she understood and would be there whenever he returned to The Falls.

It wasn't four months after he'd put a ring on her finger that she changed from the carefree, light-hearted woman with whom he had fallen in love to someone who wouldn't talk or let him touch her. He'd lain next to his wife for ten days and in all that time, she would turn her back on him whenever he attempted to make love to her. Any other man would have sought out another woman for physical release but Aiden could not and would not cheat on Denise. He would leave her first before breaking his vow to commit his fidelity, honor and his trust.

He continued to stare at Taryn, unable to believe her boyfriend had cheated on her *and* with her best friend. Although she'd been hurt, the duplicity had not broken her. She continued to go to work and conducted herself like the professional she'd been trained to be.

It hadn't taken him long to realize Taryn possessed all of the qualities he liked in a woman and would've wanted in a wife. She had a wonderful sense of humor, which made him laugh—something that had been missing in his life for a couple of years. He'd found her patient, but firm if necessary when it came to his children. His girls now picked up after themselves, set and cleared the table and had stopped protesting when it came time for them to go to bed. And that patience extended to him when he tried and failed to remember a dance step.

Last Sunday, she'd announced she was going to church and if anyone would like to go with her. Allison and Livia hadn't hesitated when they raced upstairs to get dressed. The decision to attend services came a bit more slowly for Aiden. The last time he'd attended his local church was to baptize Livia. He'd felt a little strange sitting in the pew for the first time in years. Not much in the ninety-year-old house of worship had changed since he'd attended Sunday school as a boy, married and baptized his children.

After services ended, they headed for Ruthie's for brunch and then went home, where the girls watched a movie. He and Taryn worked side by side in the kitchen; he prepared dinner and lunch for the following day, while she baked a batch of shortbread cookies.

What shocked Aiden into silence was Allison whispering in his ear that she wanted Miss Taryn to become her new momma because she didn't yell like her old momma. He did not want to believe that the lasting memory his then three-year-old daughter had of her mother was shrieking.

"Fletcher, I'm ready for another," Aiden announced, raising his cup.

Lucas got up and walked over to the chafing dishes to refill his plate. "You keep drinking that Jack, little bro, and you're going down for the count."

"I'm drinking Jim not Jack, big brother. And because I'm not driving tonight, it's all good."

Esther shook her head. "You boys ought to stop before you see the three kings."

"Who are the three kings?" Tommy asked.

"Jim Beam, Jack Daniels and Johnny Walker."

"Well, damn," he said under his breath, eliciting chuckles from those sitting close enough to overhear him.

Jonah stood and joined Luke at the serving tables. "I gave up the hard stuff a long time ago."

Rebecca, or Becky, a nickname that followed her into adulthood, rolled her eyes at her husband. "That's because you probably were sipping some of that hooch your granddaddy used to make, and it ate a hole in your cast-iron belly."

Jonah turned and glared at his bride of forty years. "Aw, come on, Becky. You know we Gibsons are now legit."

"What's this about the family making moonshine?" Tommy questioned.

Jonah threw up a hand. "Now, Becky, why did you have to go and bring that up? And if the truth be known, it was your grandpappy and his brothers who were our best customers."

Aiden decided it was time to end the conversation. "Enough talk about hooch. Don't forget we have kids here who are like mynah birds and repeat everything they hear."

As if on cue, Lucas's sons jumped up from their table. "Daddy, can we go in the backyard and play?"

"Isn't it getting dark?"

"The lights come on automatically at dusk," Aiden announced.

"Pull-eeeze!" chorused the other children at the table.

Luke shared a look with his wife, who nodded. "Okay. But you have to put your coats on."

Jonah returned to the table and set down his plate. "You outdid yourself with the brisket, Aiden. I want you to think about becoming the Den's designated pit master."

Aiden chewed and swallowed a mouthful of coleslaw. Assuming the responsibility of pit master meant he wouldn't have to work six days a week, or the night shift, and could share dinner with his daughters. "I'll definitely think about it."

Taryn grasped Aiden's hand as he assisted her to sit next to him on the top step to the porch. She had gone into the house to put on a sweater over her T-shirt. The temperature had dropped a few degrees from the midforties to just above freezing. It was past midnight and the house was quiet. Sharleen had left before the halftime entertainment with his sister-in-law Minna, Esther and their children. There was a lot of whining and grumbling because they didn't want to go home, but had to be reminded that they had to get up and go to school the next day. The men lingered after the game ended to load tables, benches and chafing dishes into the restaurant's van, while Jessica had helped Taryn pack up leftovers for the families with children.

She rested her against Aiden's shoulder. "It was a wonderful get-together."

His arm tightened around her waist. "I believe it came off okay."

Tilting her chin, she looked up at him. "It was more than okay. The food was delicious and everyone seemed to enjoy themselves."

"They did, despite the references to my folks making hooch."

Taryn bit back a smile. "I saw Tommy's face when Becky mentioned your great-granddaddy making moonshine and I thought he was going to choke on his food. It's apparent someone didn't clue him in on past family secrets."

"Well, after tonight, I'm sure Becky will tell him everything." Aiden stretched out his legs and crossed his sock-covered feet at the ankles. "He really shouldn't be that shocked because most families have buried secrets they don't want to dig up."

"Amen," Taryn said softly.

"Are you saying the Robinsons also have secrets they'd rather not talk about?"

"No comment."

"Come on, beautiful. You can tell me and it will go no further than this porch."

"I'll tell you about it at another time. Livia's birthday is coming up in two weeks, and have you decided how you want to celebrate it?" Taryn asked, shifting the tone of the conversation away from her.

"Yes. I want to take her to Medieval Times in Hanover, Maryland."

"Are you going to make it a day trip?"

"No," Aiden said. "I plan for us to stay overnight."

"She's going to love it."

Aiden stared at Taryn as she smiled at him. "You've been there?"

She nodded. "One year, I accompanied several fifth grade classes for their class trip to the one in New Jersey. It was an amazing experience for everyone."

"Did the kids like it?"

"They loved it, and I loved it."

"Are you coming with us?" Aiden questioned.

Taryn stared at the porch lights on the house across the road, complete shock freezing her features. Had Aiden asked her to travel out of the state with him and his children to gauge her reaction, or was he truly serious about involving her in what would become a family outing.

What Aiden did not realize was she wasn't family and realistically could not become a part of his family. She only wanted to be his daughters' teacher, not their mother. And forming a personal attachment with Allison and Livia, and then having to leave them after a year or two was certain to be emotionally traumatic, not only for the girls but also for her. She'd grown fond of her students and looked forward to interacting them. They were bright, engaging and eager to learn new things. Everyday had become an adventure for them when introducing them to an unfamiliar concept or discussing the books during their read-aloud sessions.

"I don't think so," she said, shaking her head at the same time. "You enjoy your time with your daughters." Easing out his embrace, she stood up and he rose with her. "It's time I go in and get ready for bed."

Aiden rested his hands on her shoulders, bringing her closer. "You know the girls want you to come. I plan to rent a suite with adjoining bedrooms where you and the girls can have a sleepover."

A hint of a smile touched the corners of Taryn's mouth. "If I have a sleepover with them, none of us will get any sleep. I remember sleepovers with my friends and we'd stay up all night laughing and talking, and then we couldn't get up the next morning."

"You won't have to get up early. The first show isn't until 4:30, and the last show begins at 7:00. I just want to make this birthday a special one for Livia because she's been talking nonstop about this birthday. You don't have to give me a firm answer tonight. Just promise me you'll think about it."

"Okay, Aiden. I'll think about."

Taryn did not have time to react when Aiden's hands went from her shoulders to cradle her face. Jessica saw what Taryn hadn't wanted to acknowledge and what she had denied from the first time Aiden walked into her bedroom to see her in the revealing top. Aiden wanted her and she wanted him, if only to remind her that she was a woman who'd missed sharing her body with a man.

His head came down seemingly in slow motion and brushed his mouth over hers in a kiss that was as soft as the gossamer wings of a butterfly. As if testing her response, he increased the pressure until her lips parted. Taryn inhaled his warm breath when he staked his claim. His kiss was shocking and intoxicating at the same time. The mere feel of his mouth on hers had sent her pulses racing, while reminding her of how it had been since she'd felt desirable. Then it ended as quickly as it had begun.

Turning on her heel, she walked into the house without a backward glance to see if Aiden was following and closed the storm door behind her, and headed for her bedroom. Her mind was spinning out of control at the same time her emotions toward Aiden were reeling in confusion. Although they resided under the same roof, she did not get to see that much of him. She was in bed when he returned from his night shift, and as promised, he'd prepare breakfast, lunch and dinner for them and store the meals in labeled containers in the refrigerator. It was only when he was on the every two week rotating day shift that he was home in time to share dinner with them. Once his children were in bed, she was able to continue their twice-weekly, half hour dance lessons. Occasionally their lessons would become sexually charged when Aiden dipped her, his mouth only inches from hers, but it would end before he kissed her. These were the times when she wanted him to kiss, because Taryn found it harder and harder to ignore her traitorous fantasies.

Aiden kissing her was a blatant reminder of what she had missed and, more importantly, what she needed. She wanted and needed him to make love to her, if only to assuage the memory of a man she had forgiven but couldn't forget the hateful words he flung at her after she found him in bed with her best friend. Words she had never repeated to anyone—not even Jessica.

You can't get involved with him, the silent voice whispered in her head. Taryn knew getting romantically involved with Aiden would not end well—at least not for her. He'd asked her whether she would join him in celebrating Livia's birthday and she decided she would, only because she didn't want to disappoint the child.

Stripping off her clothes, she walked into the bathroom, stood under the shower and let the warm water sluice over her head and body. If it hadn't been so late, she definitely would've called Jessica and bared her soul. In the past, it had been Aisha to whom she'd told her innermost secrets, who in turn confided those to James.

She turned off the water and wrapped her head in a

towel and another around her body to absorb the moisture. Taryn skipped her nightly ritual of slathering a moisturizer over her damp skin when she pulled a nightgown over her head, got into bed, slipped under the sheet and pulled the comforter up to her neck. She tossed and turned restlessly until exhaustion won out and enveloped her in a deep, dreamless sleep.

Chapter Ten

Taryn walked into the kitchen a week later, coming to a complete stop when she saw Aiden leaning into the refrigerator. The fabric of a white T-shirt strained across his broad shoulders as he reached inside. Taryn couldn't pull her eyes away from the relaxed jeans riding low on his hips and displaying a hint of his briefs' waistband. She'd seen enough boxers and briefs from boys who refused to pull up their pants to last her a lifetime, yet it was different with Aiden because either his T-shirt had shrunk or it was several sizes too small to begin with.

"What are you doing up so early?" she asked softly. It wasn't quite 6:30 a.m. Aiden turned and stared at her like a deer caught in the glare of headlights. It was apparent he hadn't expected to see her as much as she hadn't expected to see him.

Holding a carton of eggs in one hand and a plastic

container filled with fresh shrimp in the other, he shouldered the refrigerator door closed. He walked across the kitchen, dipped his head and brushed a light kiss on her cheek. "Good morning, beautiful. I couldn't sleep, so I decided to get up."

"Good morning, Aiden." Taryn managed to hide her reaction to his chaste kiss and him calling her beautiful. It was only the second time he'd kissed her since the night of Super Bowl Sunday and for that she was grateful. "I didn't think you'd be up this early after working last night."

"I could say the same thing about you getting up so early, because you don't work nights. What's the matter? You couldn't sleep?"

"I kept waking up," she said truthfully. Dreams, disturbing and erotic, had her tossing and turning most of the night until she decided to get up.

"Do you always have trouble sleeping?" Aiden asked.

"Not normally."

"What time did you go to bed?"

"It was probably a little after nine. I'd tried watching TV, but found that I couldn't keep my eyes open. Next thing I know the television was watching me. I turned it off and tried going back to sleep, but then I kept waking up."

"That only happens to me when I'm overly stimulated," Aiden admitted. "It's as if my brain refuses to shut down until I pass out from exhaustion." He paused, smiling. "What you see standing before you is the Wolf Den's newest pit master."

Taryn's eyebrows lifted. "Which means what?"

"I'll work an average of three to four days a week

instead of six. Jonah talked about cutting my hours because I don't see my kids enough."

"What about Lucas? Is he going to cut back his hours, too?"

"No. The difference between me and Luke is that his kids have their mother and father, while I'm a single parent. Fletcher has finally agreed to leave his job at the used car dealership to come on full-time after the owner decreased his hours for the second time over the last four months. It will take him a little while to get used to working in the kitchen but I have no doubt he'll learn quickly. With Jonah, Tommy, Luke and now Fletcher, we'll have four full-time cooks rotating between the day and night shifts. Sharleen is still able to handle the lunch crowd, while her daughter and niece come in for the night folks. Sharleen's brother, who just retired after working twenty-five years as a telephone lineman, has agreed to tend bar."

"You guys are really keeping it in the family," Taryn teased.

"I told you, we had to learn the hard way not to bring in outsiders who were stealing us blind. This is not to say family won't steal from family, but at the end of the year, everyone gets a nice bonus check based on the year's profits. And if the Den goes under, then we're all out of jobs."

"What are your responsibilities as pit master?"

"I'll go around ten at night, prep the meats and load up the smoker for them to cook overnight."

"How many hours does it take for them to cook?"

"If I set the temperature at two hundred degrees, then it should take ten to twelve hours."

Taryn walked over to the coffeemaker to brew a pot. "How much meat do you smoke at any given time?"

Aiden emptied the container of shrimp into a strainer and rinsed them with cold water. "It all depends. Ribs, brisket and pork shoulder are always on the menu, so I'll put on twenty-five to thirty pounds of ribs, a dozen pork shoulders, at least twenty chickens and probably about fifteen pounds of brisket every other day."

"That's a lot of meat."

"You're in the South, Taryn, and we're known to like our meat. If we don't sell out the meat on the second day, then it's donated to the church's soup kitchen, along with leftovers from the day's specials."

"I like that," Taryn said. "It's a sin to throw away food when so many people are starving."

"You're preaching to the choir, Taryn."

"Would you like a cup of coffee?"

He nodded. "Please."

Taryn waited for the brewing cycle to finish and filled a mug stamped with *The World's Greatest Dad*. "Do you want it black or with milk?" She knew Aiden never added sugar to his coffee.

"A little milk, please."

Taryn retrieved a container of milk, added a splash to his cup and handed it to him before filling a mug for herself. She peered into the sink. "Are you making shrimp and grits this morning?"

"Yep. I thought I'd surprise you, but now you know."

Taryn's eyes lit up like a child seeing a gaily-wrapped gift under the tree for the first time on Christmas morning. "I could kiss you!"

Aiden's hands continued peeling shrimp as he met her eyes. "I wouldn't mind if you did."

She sobered quickly at his invitation. "No, Aiden," she whispered. "We're not going to do that when your kids can see us." His blue-green orbs bored into her like heated lasers.

"I would never disrespect you by letting my kids see us in a compromising situation that would send them mixed messages. When I kissed you Super Bowl Sunday, it was something I'd wanted to do for a while. You're beautiful, intelligent and even though you try to downplay it, you're sexy as hell. And I know if circumstances were different between us, I'd definitely date you."

Her expression didn't change, although her heart was pumping as fast as a hummingbird's wings. Aiden had just verbalized what his eyes had been saying all along. He wanted her, while what they both wanted was impossible. "But the circumstances aren't different because I work *for* you, and I've made it a practice not to get involved with anyone I work with."

Washing and drying his hands, he approached her. "Have I ever treated you like an employee or even a coworker?"

"No, but—"

"No buts, Taryn," he said, cutting off what she wanted to say. "From the very first day you moved in, I've related to you on equal footing. The only difference is I pay you to look after my children."

"But that still makes me your employee," she argued.

"That's true, Taryn, but I'm simply making it known that I like you in the way a man likes a woman and *if* things were different between us, I would show you just how much I like you."

Taryn couldn't stop the wave of heat moving from

her chest to her face. She'd misjudged Aiden. Her mouth opened and closed several times as she tried forming the words that wouldn't make her sound like a complete idiot. "I'm sorry, Aiden, for misinterpreting your intent."

Aiden nodded as his mouth curved into an unconscious smile. "I accept your apology. And even though I want to apologize for kissing you last week, that would be a lie."

Much to her surprise, Taryn laughed. "And it would be a lie if I said I didn't enjoy it."

His smile widened. "So the lady does like me just a little bit."

"The lady likes you more than a little bit. You're an incredible father, a wonderful cook and you're becoming quite the dancer. And I enjoy being with you, yet I can't allow myself to think of us going beyond friendship."

Aiden's eyes darkened with an unnamed emotion as he continued to stare at her.

"I know you're concerned about you being my employee," he finally said after a swollen silence. "And I'd never use that to take advantage of you. I also wouldn't cheat on you, because I've never cheated on any woman with whom I've been involved. That also includes my ex-wife."

There was something in Aiden's eyes and voice that indicated vulnerability; it was the first time Taryn couldn't detect the confidence and inner strength that had sustained him as a SEAL. She moved closer, wrapped her arms around his waist, rested her cheek against his chest and counted the strong steady beats of his heart.

"You could never be like him."

* * *

Aiden buried his face in Taryn's sweet-smelling hair. Her shampoo reminded him of a field of wildflowers. He wanted to tell Taryn he was falling in love with her but feared her rejecting him again. He wanted to tell her she wouldn't be the first woman to become involved with her boss and she definitely wouldn't be the last. While she related to him as the one who signed her paycheck, it wasn't the same with him. To him, she wasn't an employee, but a woman who embodied everything he wanted in a lover and eventually a wife.

His brother and uncle had urged him to start dating again, while his sister had tried setting him up with some of her friends who'd expressed an interest in him. His response was always the same: he did not want to take time away from his daughters.

Taryn wanted friendship, while he wanted more, but if that was all she was willing to offer, then he would accept it. "I'll take friendship." *For now,* he added silently.

Taryn unpacked her overnight bag, putting things away in dresser drawers after lining them with butcher paper and then repeated the action with Allison's and Livia's, as the two girls sat on a loveseat watching cartoons.

Aiden had waited until everyone was seated and belted in the Suburban before he announced to his daughters that they were going to a medieval castle to watch a jousting tournament. Both girls appeared puzzled until Taryn pulled the Medieval Times's website up on her phone to give them an idea of what they could expect to see. Viewing the images on the phone had both girls babbling excitedly about knights on horses. They'd watched enough animated movies to know knights wore suits of armor and fought one another while on horseback.

They'd left The Falls at eight that morning and entered Baltimore's city limits around two in the afternoon. Aiden had stopped once to pull off the road to purchase lunch from a drive-through restaurant, while reminding his daughters not to eat too much because they were scheduled to eat around five.

He'd reserved adjoining suites at a hotel in Hanover that was accessible to downtown Baltimore, historic Annapolis and Baltimore's Inner Harbor. Taryn felt as if she'd stepped back in time to when she'd attended college and spent time shopping in the Arundel Mills mall and strolling Baltimore's harbor after overindulging on crab cakes. She'd just placed a bag with gifts for Livia and Allison on a shelf in the closet when Aiden walked into her bedroom suite.

"Do you need me to call the front desk for anything?"

Taryn smiled at him over her shoulder. "No. We have everything we'll need." Her room had two full beds, bedside tables with lamps, floor lamps, a desk with ports for a computer, and an armoire with a flat screen. "How's your room?"

Aiden ran a hand over the stubble covering his head. "It's really nice."

She walked over to the window and stared at the empty outdoor pool. "Coming here is nostalgic for me."

"Why?" Aiden asked as he moved behind her.

Taryn shivered slightly when she detected his breath on her ear. Things had changed between them after her misinterpreting his intentions toward her. She no longer regarded him as her employer but her friend—

friends without benefits. His revised responsibilities and work hours permitted him more time to spend with his daughters. Allison and Livia were able to read several picture books now and were eager to show their father how much they'd learned when he set aside time after dinner to read with them.

"When I attended Howard, I'd come to Baltimore whenever I had a craving for crabs."

"Did you enjoy your college experience?"

She nodded. "I loved it. Whenever I didn't have classes or babysitting there was always something to see or somewhere to go. Most times, I either hung out in museums or sought out new restaurants offering student discounts."

"Were you a struggling college student?"

"Not really. My parents didn't have to pay for my brother's college because he was accepted into the Naval Academy, which meant the money they saved covered my tuition at Howard. My parents gave me a monthly budget and if I went over, then I ate ramen noodles until they deposited more money into my checking account. That's why I decided to get a part-time job babysitting. The money I earned paid for the little extras."

"Did you have a car?"

"Not the first two years. Once I became a junior and moved off campus, my father bought a secondhand car for me that was a couple of rungs above a hoopty. Daddy said he didn't expect me to drive between DC and New York because it had too many miles on the odometer but it was good enough to take me from my apartment to the campus. Students would pile in if they wanted me to drive them somewhere and the only requisite was everyone had to chip in for gas."

Taryn had Aiden laughing hysterically when she revealed the episode with her and Jessica eating at a fancy restaurant and paying for a meal that wouldn't fill up a bird. "We went back to our apartment and searched through seat cushions, handbags and coat pockets for loose change. We finally came up with enough money, including the little we had left after settling the check, to go to a chicken joint and ordered a bucket with half a dozen biscuits. We ate our fill and then stored the rest in the fridge for breakfast."

"You and Jessica experienced what I want for Allie and Livia when they finally go to college."

"Eating ramen when they run out of money?" Taryn teased.

"Yes, if it means they won't go hungry. I want to provide them with the opportunity to choose to be whatever they want, and that's going to happen if I plan for their future."

Taryn turned and saw what she interpreted as determination in his eyes. "Isn't that what you're doing, Aiden? You hired me to help give your children the foundation they need to begin their education, and they're learning new things at an alarming rate. Once they're enrolled in school, they'll be able to keep up with their peers with little or no effort. Plus, they should be able to hold their own against those attempting to bully them. It wasn't nice, but I wanted to applaud Allison for standing up to her cousin. Most girls her age would've been hesitant to say anything in a room filled with adults."

"That was before you came. There was a time when I could hardly get Allie to say anything without prompting her to speak. It was Livia who'd become her spokesperson, and I think it was because Allie may have remembered things her mother did or said that had her traumatized. You've become a positive force in both their lives, Taryn, and for that I'll be eternally grateful."

She shook her head. "I can't take all of the credit. Whatever you see in your daughters was always there, I just help to bring it out." Taryn wanted to ask Aiden if he had considered having Allison see a therapist to possibly address some underlying issues resulting from her parents' turbulent relationship because she did have memories of her mother's outbursts.

A frown formed between his eyes as a muscle twitched noticeably in his jaw. "Why can't you just accept a compliment?"

"It's not about accepting compliments, Aiden."

"If not, then what is it?"

"You've called me a miracle worker when I'm nothing of the sort. I've been trained to teach and when children learn, they are able to develop confidence when it comes to reading a book, writing their names or counting. Knowledge is power and once they obtain it, no one can take it from them. Allison and Livia have above average intelligence that must be carefully nurtured so they can excel, and if they chose to become president of the United States, astronauts or neurosurgeons, then it shouldn't be beyond their imagination. Even after I stop being their teacher and you choose to continue to homeschool them until they're ready for middle school, then make certain their new teacher will continue to build on what I've begun."

Aiden stared at Taryn under lowered lids. "What if I don't want a new teacher?"

"Then you'll have to enroll them in either public or

a private school. Remember, you do have a couple of choices."

"You're right," he said after a noticeable pause. "I think it's time we head out now because I don't know how long it will take us to park."

"I'm almost finished here. What I don't put away now I'll do once we get back."

Aiden watched his daughters react with wild abandon to the knights on horses galloping across the arena as they cheered on their yellow knight. They were seated in the first row with an unobstructed view of the nonstop action. Before they were seated, they'd posed for photos with the queen and for a group picture with him and Taryn.

Initially, they were squeamish having to eat with their hands as was the custom during the medieval time period. But after drinking their soup and biting into the delicious chicken, they attacked the meal with relish. Aiden knew Taryn was right about it being exciting because he found himself cheering along with the others in their section as the knights dismounted from Lipizzaners, pure Spanish stallions, to engage in ferocious swordplay. He marveled at the actors' ability to ride and fall off their mounts and emerge uninjured. The highlight of the event was when the royal falconer released the falcon out into the arena, only to have the bird return to land on his gloved hand.

With wide eyes, and seemingly unable to move, Livia stared at the bird as it flew over her head. Once the falcon returned to his handler and his head was covered with the leather hood, the color returned to her cheeks as she jumped and screamed excitedly. Aiden couldn't help but smile when he saw how much his daughters were enjoying themselves. It was one thing for them to play with their cousins and another to go out and enjoy an experience that would last them for years. It had taken him days of searching the internet for events and venues for a child's birthday and when he saw the medieval dinner and tournament, he knew he'd hit the jackpot. Aiden knew he couldn't go back and relive the first five years of their lives, many in which he hadn't seen them for months, but he would make certain to be in their lives for the next five and the five thereafter, until they were independent adults.

The show concluded and they wended their way through the crowd and out into the parking lot. Falling sleet had covered the windshields of cars and accumulated on tree branches. Reaching into the pocket of his peacoat, Aiden pulled out his daughters' knitted caps. "You girls have to take your crowns off and put these on and then wait here for me to bring the Suburban around."

Turning up the collar to his coat, Aiden jogged to where he'd parked the SUV. It took nearly five minutes before he was able to maneuver out of his spot to where Taryn, Allison and Livia waited. They got in quickly and sighed in unison.

"It's nice and warm in here," Livia said, as she removed her cap and shook it out, icy particles hitting Allison's face.

"Hey! You're wetting me up," Allison said in protest.

Livia looked at her sister. "I'm sorry."

Aiden glanced over his shoulder to see whether his daughters had secured their seat belts before driving out of the crowded parking lot. He winked at Taryn when she took off her ski cap and combed her fingers through her hair. He'd gotten so used to seeing her hair in a ponytail that he was pleasantly surprised to find that she'd left it loose.

"You were right."

Taryn gave him a questioning look. "What about?"

"The tournament was wonderful."

She nodded. "I knew you would like it."

Aiden was finally able to drive out of the parking lot onto the street leading back to the hotel. "The food was delicious."

"The chicken was good, Daddy," Livia said from the second row of seats.

"Yes it was, sweetie. What did you like, Allie?"

"The chicken and the bread."

Livia, leaning as far as her seat belt would permit, tapped the back of Aiden's seat. "What I really liked was our yellow knight winning and getting to meet the princess."

Aiden shared a smile with Taryn as the two girls chatted excitedly about what they liked. The short trip ended with him pulling into the lot to the hotel. He cut off the engine, got out and helped Taryn down, and then his daughters. Guests were milling around the lobby, waiting to check in, as they walked to the elevator.

Allison tugged on his sleeve. "Daddy, do we have to go to bed now?"

"No, baby. You and your sister can stay up because we're not going back until tomorrow morning."

Taryn ushered the two girls toward their bedroom. "Come, let's change into something more comfortable. But first I want you to take a shower and put on your pajamas."

"Me first," Allison announced loudly as she raced Livia into their bedroom.

Taryn sat on the sofa next to Aiden, while Livia and Allison occupied the loveseat opening gaily-wrapped gifts. She'd showered, changed into sweats and presented both girls with gift bags.

Livia gasped audibly when she opened a small velvet box. She slipped off the loveseat. "Daddy, look what Miss Taryn gave me!"

"They are beautiful." There was no mistaking the awe in his voice.

Taryn didn't have time to react when Livia threw her arms around her neck and hugged her. "Thank you for the earrings, Miss Taryn."

She kissed the chubby cheek. "You're very welcome." Aiden's daughters wore tiny gold hoops in their pierced lobes, and she'd purchased a pair of small diamond studs with screw backs for Livia. Her grandmother had given her a pair of diamond studs when she graduated high school, and because of the total caret weight, she only wore them on special occasions.

"Look what I got!" Allison squealed in excitement. She held up a gold necklace with a capital *A*. She scrambled off the loveseat and launched herself at Taryn. "Thank you, Miss Taryn. I love it."

"I missed your birthday in December, so I decided to get you something," Taryn explained and kissed the dark curls.

"I love my necklace."

She smiled at the child. "I'm glad you do." Taryn watched as Allison and Livia ran out of the sitting area and into their bedroom.

Aiden, threading his fingers through Taryn's, pressed his mouth to her ear. "You really didn't have to give them anything," he whispered in her ear.

Taryn turned to look at him, noticing the length of his gray lashes resting on high cheekbones. "I know, but I wanted to give them a little something."

"What you gave them was more than a little something."

"We love big and small jewelry and it doesn't matter whether we're little or big girls."

He kissed her ear. "And you've made my little girls very, very happy."

Taryn pulled back, allowing for a modicum of space between her and Aiden. "That's because I enjoy being with them." She had consciously attempted not to relate to Allison and Livia as their mother, but with each passing day, she found it more difficult not to think of them as her daughters.

"I know you probably don't want to hear it, but you've changed me inside and out. I'd told myself I didn't need someone to share my life with because there wasn't enough room to let them in. That having Allie and Livia is enough. My uncle gets on my case when he says I should start dating again. Been there, done that. And I don't want to interview women before I introduce them to my daughters."

"You interviewed me," Taryn reminded him.

"I didn't interview you to sleep with you."

Her eyebrows lifted. "Are you saying if you have a relationship with a woman, then you would expect to sleep with her?"

Aiden nodded. "That would be the only reason. However, it would be different with you."

"Why me, Aiden? What makes me different from other women?"

"We would date each other and I would not sleep with you unless you want me to."

Taryn looked at him as if he'd taken leave of his senses. "You want me to assume responsibility of saying yea or nay?" He nodded. "Why me?" she repeated.

His gaze bore into hers. "I don't want you to believe I'm taking advantage of you."

"You won't because I'd never allow you to take advantage of me." She paused and lowered her eyes. "It hasn't been easy for me living with you because you're a constant reminder of what I once had and what is now missing in my life, and that is intimacy. But I will not sleep with you or any other man because I'm horny. I have to have more."

"And the more is someone you can trust not to cheat on you."

Leaning closer, Aiden kissed the end of her nose. "Weren't you the one who said, without trust there is no love?"

A wry smile touched her lips. "I do remember saying something like that."

"I know you're not in love with me, and you may never fall in love with me, but there's no reason why we can't have fun."

Taryn did not want to believe Aiden was offering her something no man with whom she had been involved had suggested. She had a choice in where to take their relationship. "Why does it sound as if we're negotiating a deal?"

"Because relationships, like teamwork, involve discussions and arriving at a mutual decision."

She closed her eyes as a heavy silence filled the room. Aiden hadn't touched her intimately, yet she could feel an increasing shiver of gentle desire coursing through her. Taryn had continued to tell herself not to get involved with Aiden, to ignore the virility coming off him in waves and to deny the strong passions within her that kept her from a restful night's sleep.

Shifting slightly, Taryn buried her face between his neck and shoulder. "I don't want you to view me as a spurned woman who can't get over her ex."

"Are you over him?"

"Yes."

"Then that settles it, Taryn. You or I don't have to bring him up again."

"Okay." She didn't see Aiden smile when he pressed a kiss to her hair, but she felt it.

"We'll have some time to ourselves during the spring break."

"What's happening then?" she asked.

"My mother and stepfather are inviting all of their grandchildren to come down to Florida for the week. If you want to go somewhere during that week, then let me know and I'll tell Jonah I'm taking time off for vacation."

Taryn mentally estimated she had almost two months before she would be willing to go from being Aiden's friend to his lover. Unknowingly, he had pinpointed the timeframe she'd set for herself whenever she agreed exclusively to date one man.

Smiling, she extended her hand. "Deal."

Aiden stared at her outstretched hand for thirty seconds before he took it and dropped a kiss on her knuckles. "Deal."

Chapter Eleven

Aiden tightened his hold on his daughters' hands as he led them into the high school gymnasium for the annual Father/Daughter Dance. Music blared from a powerful sound system as girls, ranging in age from toddlers to teens, danced with their fathers to the Bee Gees classic hit "Staying Alive." The gym had been transformed into an ethereal forest with tubs of artificial trees, palms, flowers and life-like birds suspended from the ceiling by wires.

A refreshment station was set up along one wall, and teachers were busy ladling punch into plastic cups, while others were handing out cookies, bags of popcorn and cotton candy. It had been nearly twenty years since he'd entered his old school, and the first time for Allison and Livia. He knew they were anxious about going to the dance, until Taryn helped them into their costumes.

When Taryn had first shown him the sketches of what she intended to make, he'd been unable to speak for several minutes. The drawings were reminiscent of those by Hollywood and Broadway costume designers. She admitted that as a girl she'd sit and watch her grandfather meticulously sew tiny stitches into the fabric, which would eventually become the lapel for a man's suit. He also taught her to sketch a design, make the pattern and lastly, sew the garment.

She had turned Livia into a sparkling green fairy with gossamer wings bedazzled with minute green-and-white pastes. The elastic used to loop the wings over her shoulders was an exact match for her tights, leotard and ballet slippers. A feathery mask in the same hue completed her ethereal outfit.

Allison had become a woodland elf, replete with pointed ears, a green double-breasted jacket, matching cap, candy cane striped tights, and green slippers with exaggerated pointed toes. Taryn had designed a red lace mask with green ties for her face.

Aiden felt a measure of pride when curious stares were directed at him and his girls as they made their way across the gymnasium to where Fletcher stood with his daughters. He and his brother-in-law exchanged rough embraces, while his nieces greeted their cousins with squeals of excitement. Eight-year-old Danielle and six-year-old Ava were dressed as gnomes. Fletcher Tompkins, tall and slightly built, was graying prematurely and joked he would probably be completely white before he turned forty. His quick smile and laughing hazel eyes put everyone at ease as soon as they met him.

"Your girls look as if they're ready for a movie set,"

Fletcher shouted in order to be heard over the blast-ing music.

"I have to thank Taryn for that," Aiden said close to Fletcher's ear. "She made their costumes. By the way, is the music too loud or are we getting old?"

Fletcher shook his head. "They say if it's too loud, then you're too old."

Aiden nodded. Fletcher hadn't grown up in Wickham Falls but in the neighboring town of Mineral Springs. Fletcher had played high school basketball and when-ever his school played Johnson County High, he looked for Esther in the stands and blew her a kiss. His arro-gance infuriated many of the boys from The Falls be-cause Mineral Springs was their fiercest rivals. Fletcher enlisted in the army, trained as a mechanic and, after five years, returned home to take up with Esther, who'd promised to wait for him.

Danielle tugged on Fletcher's arm. "Daddy, can I go and get something to drink?"

Fletcher nodded. "Yes. And take Ava, Livia and Al-lison with you." He waited until the girls were out of earshot to pull Aiden into a corner where they couldn't be overheard. "I didn't expect to see you here. What made you change your mind?"

Aiden stared down at the toes of his spit-shined boots. "I decided it's time I stop shielding my girls from things they should be exposed to. The Father/Daugh-ter Dance is a longtime tradition here in The Falls and they have a right to celebrate it along with every other girl. I can't control what folks say about their mother and her family, but I will protect them whenever I can." His head popped up and he gave Fletcher a steady stare. "The boys in The Falls were ready to kick your ass whenever you came here to play because they claimed you disrespected them by coming on to one of their girls, but you didn't let it stop you. Well, I'm not going to let people label my children where they eventually become self-fulfilling prophesies."

"I don't think you'll have to worry too much about your girls, Aiden. They're feisty and independent."

He had to agree with Fletcher. Since Taryn had come to live with them, it was as if they'd come into their own. Their personalities were more defined and they were becoming individuals who were not afraid to express their emotions.

Aiden had suggested to Taryn she plan something for them to do together the week Allison and Livia were in Florida. His excitement to spend a week alone was short-lived, however, when she told him she wanted to go to New York to see her family, after her mother called to say she missed her. The change in their relationship was so subtle that it had surprised them both. Not only were they spending more time together but Aiden felt comfortable and confident enough to touch and kiss Taryn and have her reciprocate. However, he was careful to stop before making love, because he knew she did not feel comfortable having sex while the children were in the house. Aiden also knew he had to move slowly with Taryn because it was something he had come to regret with Denise. He hadn't taken the time to know his ex-wife until it was too late.

Taryn was a constant reminder of what had been missing in his life—a normal relationship with a woman. They'd become a family unit in every sense. They lived under the same roof, shared meals, watched television, played board games, attended church services and enjoyed extended family get-togethers.

But Taryn's presence in his life still had the potential to be only temporary. Aiden had experienced unease when Taryn returned home from her monthly Friday night gathering with Jessica and the other teachers from the district and admitted she missed the camaraderie that came from working in a school building. He'd given her a contract with a clause that she could opt out thirty days before the end of the calendar year. He refused to think of her not renewing the contract because not only did his children need her but so did he.

"They are really coming into their own," he said in agreement.

"You know, I've been talking about me and Esther saving to buy a bigger house because we want another baby." Aiden nodded. "Well, we're going to get a larger house but it's not in The Falls. My folks want something smaller, so we're going to exchange homes. They're moving here and I'm moving the family to Mineral Springs."

Aiden didn't realize he'd been holding his breath. "So you're going back home."

"You can say that. My girls will root for Mineral Springs, while yours will cheer for The Falls. It's like history repeating itself. Maybe one of your girls will fall for a Mineral Springs guy like I did with your sister."

"Don't even go there, brother. I don't want to think about Allie and Livia dating."

"You'll be like Mr. T. and say, 'I pity the fool' that messes with my daughter."

Aiden laughed. "You've got that right." He had at least another ten or twelve years before he had to concern himself with his daughters going out with a boy. "When's the move?"

"This Sunday. My brothers have offered to come and switch out the bedroom furniture. Everything else stays. And when your girls come over, they'll have a nice big yard in which to play."

A teacher-chaperone approached them. "This is a father/daughter celebration, so I expect all fathers to dance with their girls."

Fletcher rested an arm over Aiden's shoulder. "You heard the lady. Let's go and dance."

Aiden whispered a silent thanks to Taryn for the lessons when he was able to follow the steps for several line dances. He did double-duty dancing with his daughters at the same time whenever the pace of the music slowed to ballads.

During an intermission, all of the girls were directed to line up by costume category. Aiden felt his chest swell with pride when Livia waved to him after winning first prize for best fairy. Allison came in second for best elf, and she ran over to join him and Livia.

"I got a prize, Daddy!" She handed him an envelope.

Leaning over, he kissed Allison's forehead. "That's because you deserve a prize.

"Are you girls ready to dance some more?"

Livia shook her head. "I want to go home and show Miss Taryn my prize."

"Me, too," Allison said.

"Wait here while I tell Uncle Fletcher we're leaving."

Taryn, flanked by Allison and Livia as they sat in the parlor, shared a knowing smile with Aiden. They talked nonstop about the fun they'd had at the dance.

Both had won gift cards, and they still hadn't decided what to buy with their prize money.

Livia kicked her feet in a pair of pink fuzzy slippers. "Miss Taryn, Daddy is a real good dancer."

She feigned surprise. "Really?"

"Yup," Allison confirmed. "He knows all the steps."

Taryn returned Aiden's wink with one of her own. "That's because your Daddy is as talented as you are."

Aiden pushed to his feet. "And it's time for Daddy's girls to go to bed. Do you want me to tuck you in?"

"No!" Allison and Livia chorused.

"We are big girls, not babies," Livia added.

"I guess they told you," Taryn whispered when she and Aiden were alone.

He gave her a long penetrating stare. "I want to thank you for talking me into going to the dance."

"So you, too, had fun?"

"Yes, I did. I saw a few of the girls who hadn't been very nice to Allie and Livia."

"Did they say anything to them?"

"No. Either they were too stunned to see them there or overcome with envy when seeing our girls' costumes."

Taryn wondered if Aiden referring to his daughters as *our girls* was a Freudian slip, or had it been a deliberate gaffe. Even though she found herself falling in love with Aiden, she refused to let her heart overrule her head. He embodied everything she looked for in a man and lover, yet she still wasn't ready to go all in and surrender to her emotions.

She knew he was disappointed when she revealed that she was going to New York to visit her family during spring break but she needed to put some distance between them, if only to clear her head and view her life more objectively.

"Are you saying they were green with envy once they saw the green fairy?"

"Maybe. One father asked if I'd bought their outfits from a store specializing in costumes, and he seemed disappointed when I told him they were made expressly for them."

"Well, I'm glad they had a good time *and* won prizes."

Aiden slumped lower in his chair and stretched out his legs. "What do you have on your calendar for next weekend?"

Taryn hesitated, wondering what Aiden was planning. "Nothing. Why?"

"I'd like to take you away for a little rest and relaxation as a token of appreciation for all that you do for me and Allie and Livia."

Taryn was too startled by his suggestion to reject him outright. "Where are we going?"

"Washington, DC. I'd like you to show me where you went to college and your hangout haunts. I'll reserve suites in a hotel within walking distance to museums and art galleries."

"Okay," she agreed, since he'd said suites rather than suite. Taryn still wasn't ready to sleep with Aiden, even though she knew there would come a point where their relationship had to be resolved. Would they continue as friends or evolve to becoming friends with benefits?

Taryn checked her reflection in the mirrored doors on the closet, smoothing down the body-hugging dress over her flat belly. The neckline of the dress revealed a hint of breast with each inhalation of breath. At first, she thought the outfit a little too risqué, but dismissed it because it was too late to change into something else.

She and Aiden left The Falls at noon and checked into their hotel five hours later. He'd parked his vehicle in the hotel's underground lot and planned for them to either walk or take taxis around the city. And as promised, Aiden had reserved adjoining suites in a luxury hotel in downtown DC.

Taryn gathered the dress's matching waist-length wool jacket and crossbody bag, and had just slipped her feet into a pair of pumps when she heard the knock on the door connecting their suites. He'd planned for them to share dinner at a restaurant, specializing in steak and seafood.

"Come in." The door opened and Aiden entered resplendent in a tailored navy-blue suit, white shirt, and red, white and blue striped silk tie, and black imported slip-ons. "Wow! You look incredible!" A blush found its way up Aiden's neck with the compliment.

He extended his hands, his eyes moving slowly over her face. Taryn had taken special care with her makeup when she applied a smoky shadow to her lids, two coats of mascara on her lashes and a red-orange lipstick that enhanced the golden undertones in her brown complexion. She'd blown out her chemically-relaxed hair and, using a curling iron, styled it in a mass of curls that framed her face and bounced above her shoulders as if they'd taken on a life of their own.

Aiden took hold of her hands and pressed a kiss to her fingers. "Maybe I should cancel our dinner reservation and order room service, because I don't want some man hitting on you."

Taryn looped her arms through his. Her heels added four inches to her five-ten height. "That's not going to happen because I'm not going to take my eyes off you to see who's looking at me."

Aiden smiled, displaying a mouth of straight white teeth. "What am I going to do with you?"

Love me for an eternity, the silent voice in her head screamed. And in that moment, that's what she wanted Aiden to do. She wanted him to love her and to protect and honor their love for as long as it was humanly possible. Taryn had waged a violent war with her emotions and in the end she'd had to put up a white flag and surrender. She had kept Aiden on tenterhooks for months as to where they would take their relationship.

"I don't know, Aiden. That's a decision you'll have to make on your own."

His eyes grew wide until she was able to see the dark blue centers. "What if I want for us to be together this year, next year and every year thereafter?"

Her heart stopped and then started up in a runaway rhythm that made her feel slightly light-headed. "What are you talking about?" she whispered.

"You don't know, do you?"

"Know what, Aiden?"

"That I'm in love with you. I kept telling myself it was because I was lonely. That I hadn't been involved with a woman in so long that you had become the next best thing. Then I rationalized and told myself that I needed a mother for my children, but even that sounded hollow when I said it aloud. It's none of those things, except that I love who you are and I'm thankful and grateful that you've come into my life.

"Taryn, you're not the only one with trust issues.

I heard talk about Denise cheating on me but I didn't want to believe it. I kept telling myself it wasn't true because if she wouldn't let me make love to her then it stood to reason she wouldn't let another man touch her. Even when she left the note revealing she was leaving, I kept telling myself she would be back because mothers don't leave their children. It wasn't until after the divorce was finalized that I knew I was in some serious denial. Just when I thought I didn't have the capacity to love again, you showed up and turned my world as I knew it upside down with your beauty, intelligence and infinite patience with two little strong-willed girls who could test the patience of a saint. I don't know if you're willing to spend the rest of your life with a slightly used ex-SEAL and private military soldier, but I'm willing to wait for as long as it will take for you to give me an answer."

Taryn blinked slowly as she replayed what Aiden had just confessed. "You're asking me to marry you?"

"Yes, I am."

It was impossible for her to steady her erratic pulse as she felt Aiden's gaze boring into her as if he could see what lay in her heart. He'd admitted to loving her and she loved him, but his proposal of marriage had come out of nowhere and taken her off-guard.

"How much time do I have to think about it?"

A smile parted his firm lips. "Forever."

She leaned closer, pressing her breasts to his chest. "I never expected you to ask me to marry you. However, it's not going to take forever for me to give you an answer. I promise to let you know before my contract expires." November would give her more than enough time to know if she wanted to marry Aiden and become his children's stepmother. "Now are you going to take me to dinner or stand here and listen to my belly make strange noises?"

Aiden kissed her forehead. "Let's go, love, before we lose our table."

Aiden sat across the table in the bank-turned restaurant and stared at the woman with whom he'd bared his heart and soul. Taryn hadn't said she loved him but that did not matter. What mattered was she hadn't rejected his proposal. He hadn't planned to propose to her but was glad he'd gotten it off his chest. After all, he wasn't some adolescent boy who stuttered and stammered when he wanted to tell a girl how much he liked her.

He'd cheated death so many times that he did not have time to play games where his future was concerned. His sole focus was to provide for and protect his children and when he married, his wife would become a part of that equation. Aiden did not want to think of the unspeakable acts he had committed to earn enough money to secure his family's future but that lifestyle was in his past and he wanted to live out the rest of life without having to look over his shoulder to confront someone who wanted to retaliate for past deeds. And everything he planned with Allison and Livia they wanted to include Miss Taryn, and he loathed to think of a time when Miss Taryn wouldn't be in their lives.

"How are your seared scallops?" he asked Taryn. He'd selected a restaurant that served fish because he knew Taryn would order a seafood dish.

"Delicious. Your steak?"

"Excellent."

"One of these days I'm going to turn you into a pesca-tarian, even if it's only for one week," she said, smiling.

"I like fish, and I'm certain I'd eat it more often if we lived closer to the ocean."

Taryn dabbed the corners of her mouth with the linen napkin. "You have rivers where you can catch bass."

"True. But we would have to pay fishermen to catch them and if we can't get enough, then we can't put it on the menu."

"Do you ever add fish to the day's special?" she asked.

"Usually during the spring, we'll order crabs from the Chesapeake before they grow their hard shell and serve fried soft-shell crabs."

"I noticed you have containers of lump crabmeat in your freezer."

"I ordered those last week when Jonah placed an order because I want to experiment making crab cakes. If you have a recipe, then I'm willing to let you try it before we put in on the menu."

"Aren't you the pit master?"

"Yes," Aiden replied, "but that doesn't mean I can't introduce another dish to add to the menu."

Taryn took a sip of water. "My father is famous for his crab cakes. When I go home, I'll ask him for his recipe."

Aiden felt as if he had been punched in the gut when Taryn mentioned returning to New York. It would be the first time since her arrival that he would have the house to himself for a week. His daughters would be in Florida and Taryn in New York.

Dinner concluded with him settling the bill and es-corting Taryn out to the street where he hailed a taxi to take them back to their hotel. Once inside his suite, he slipped out of his suit jacket and tie.

"Are you ready to turn in for the night?" he asked Taryn.

"No. Let me change and wash my face and I'll see you later."

Aiden stared mutely as she walked across the room and disappeared behind the connecting door. He was galvanized into action when he picked up the phone and ordered room service before stripping down to his underwear and pulling on a pair of shorts and a T-shirt.

Taryn exchanged her dress for a tank top and cotton drawstring lounging pants, and then removed her makeup. She splashed cold water on her face before patting it dry and applying a moisturizer. Walking on bare feet, she knocked lightly on the door and pushed it open. A smile spread over her features when she saw two flutes filled with champagne and a bowl of fresh strawberries on the table in the sitting area. Aiden had left on a floor lamp and tuned the radio to a station featuring love songs.

He patted the cushion on the loveseat. "Come and sit down."

"Mr. Gibson, are you trying to seduce me?"

"Guilty as charged, Miss Robinson."

Taryn sat down, pulling her legs up under her body. "What if I seduce you first?"

Aiden draped an arm over her shoulders, pulling her closer. "I promise not to protest."

She snuggled closer. "I'm not saying we're going to do anything tonight, but if we do get reckless, I need to know if you have protection with you."

"Yes."

Taryn inhaled the lingering fragrance of Aiden's cologne mingling with his natural masculine scent and found it intoxicating. "It doesn't take me long to be under the influence," she said when he leaned over and handed her one of the flutes."

"Don't worry. I'll carry you to bed if you have a problem walking."

"I remember you carrying me to bed not too long ago," she said, reminding him of the time when they'd sat on her bed and he told her about his marriage.

"Why does that seem so long ago?" Aiden touched his flute to hers. "Here's to love and family."

"Love and family," Taryn repeated as she took a sip of the bubbly wine.

In between bites of plump strawberries and sips of champagne, she felt herself succumbing to the sensual mood enveloping her in a cocoon of longing that she did not want to escape. All of her doubts, fears and inhibitions fled when Aiden lifted her with one arm and settled her between his outstretched legs. She moaned softly when she felt the growing hardness between his thighs. Did he not know what he was doing to her?

"Aiden?"

"What is it, baby?"

Why, she thought, did his voice sound as if it had come a long way off when he'd whispered in her ear? "I need you to make love to me."

Aiden's arm tightened around her waist. "Are you certain?"

A lopsided smile curved her mouth. "I've never been more certain in my life." And she was. She had known when she got out of her car and walked up the path to

Aiden's house that their lives and future would become inexorably entwined.

Taryn felt as if she'd stepped outside of her body to watch Aiden as he carried her to his bedroom and placed her gently on the bed. The only illumination in the darkened room came from lights in outside buildings coming through partially opened drapes. She closed her eyes and let her other senses takeover.

She heard Aiden removing his clothes, then she felt his hands when he undressed her. His fingers caressed her body like a sculptor admiring his masterpiece. His hand moved up her inner thigh and she gasped. His touching her so intimately brought back long-forgotten sensual pleasure that made her want Aiden even more.

Aiden wanted to bury himself inside Taryn's soft-scented body because it had been far too long since he'd made love to a woman. However, he wanted their coming together to be special, where they would have lasting memories years from now of their first time making love to each other.

He took her mouth in a slow drugging kiss that left them moaning for more. Reaching for the condom he'd left in the drawer of the bedside table, he slipped it on and parted her legs with his knees. Holding onto his erection, he guided it into her, meeting resistance when she emitted a small cry.

"Am I hurting you?" he whispered in her ear. Aiden felt the pounding of Taryn's heart against his chest.

"No," she said breathlessly. "Just go slow."

He took his time arousing her until she was close to climaxing and as he penetrated her, his need for giving and receiving pleasure was fever-pitched. Aiden lost himself in the warmth of her body, her soft moans in his ear, and the writhing of her scented body against his. Aiden cupped her hips, pulling her even closer until they ceased to exist as separate entities, becoming one with the other. His mouth covered hers when she breathed out the last of her passions and then he released his own, the throbbing continuing until he felt slightly light-headed. It was a full sixty seconds before he garnered the strength to roll off her body. He lay on his back, staring up at the ceiling as Taryn rolled against his side and flung her arm over his belly.

"Are you okay?"

She moaned softly. "I'm wonderful. Thank you."

He smiled. She was thanking him when he should've been thanking her. "You're welcome." Aiden removed the condom and pulled the blankets up and over their bodies. Morpheus claimed them, and this was one night when both slept soundly and did not wake up until the sun was high in the sky.

DC had become a magical place for Taryn when she toured the capital city, visiting the National Museum of African American History and Culture, then returning to their hotel room to make love again. They shared a shower before going to a jazz club to listen to live music not far from the Howard University campus. She took him to a soul food restaurant for Sunday brunch of chicken and waffles.

Aiden checked out and they were on the road at one o'clock for the return drive to Wickham Falls, stopping in Mineral Springs to pick up Allison and Livia before continuing on home. Esther had given Taryn a strange look and she wondered if Aiden's sister knew that she had been sleeping with her brother.

Taryn and Aiden had agreed they would not sleep together as long as the girls were in the house; they didn't want to send them mixed signals when they believed that only mommies and daddies slept together in the same bed.

It would become their secret, and she knew it would take Herculean strength to keep her hands off Aiden whenever they were together.

Taryn's rosy world fell apart the morning she was to leave for New York when the doorbell rang. When she opened the door, she knew with a single glance that the woman was Aiden's ex-wife because of Allison's uncanny resemblance to her. Taryn realized time had not been kind to her. Her skin bore pockmarks and her complexion was sallow.

"May I help you?"

"I'm looking for my children."

"They're not here."

"When are they coming home?" Denise asked.

"It'll be a few days. I'm going to call Aiden to let him know you're here." Taryn would've invited Denise to come in but wasn't certain whether Aiden would approve. Reaching into her tote, she took out her cell phone and tapped in Aiden's number. It took less than ten seconds to tell him his ex was at the house, asking for her children. He told her not to let Denise in the house and that he was coming home.

Aiden drove as if the hounds of hell were chasing him. He refused to believe Denise would come back asking for the very children she had abandoned. He pulled into the driveway behind Taryn's SUV, tires screeching when he came to an abrupt stop. Denise, sitting on the top step of the porch, stood up at his approach.

"What the hell are you doing here?"

Rising on tiptoe, Denise got in his face. "I came to get my children."

"You don't have any children. Remember, you legally signed away your parental rights."

Denise's face crumbled like an accordion. "I was sick and I didn't know what I was doing. I want you to forgive me because I'm still in love with you and I want to see my babies."

Aiden struggled to control his temper. "I will not let you mess up my daughters' lives because you can't get yours together. Now I want you to leave my home and never come back again, or I'll get a court order to make certain you stay away." The tears streaming down Denise's face failed to move him. "Get the hell off my porch!"

He watched as the woman with whom he'd taken an oath to love and protect walked off the porch and crossed the street to get into a pickup where a man wearing a baseball cap waited. When he drove away, Aiden noticed the vehicle had Texas plates.

Turning, he stared at Taryn looking back at him. "I'm sorry you had to witness that."

"So am I," she shot back. "You were cold and heartless. Regardless of what you went through with her, Denise is still the mother of your children."

"I'm only going to warn you this one time. Do not interfere when it comes to my children."

"Interfere!" she screamed. "I'm just as involved with

your children as you are. You've asked me to marry you and to me that means I'll be Allison and Livia's stepmother, so I will have to be involved in their lives. I'm leaving now and when I come back hopefully that will give you time to come to your senses."

Chapter Twelve

Taryn left Wickham Falls with a heavy heart. She did not want to believe Aiden had warned her not to interfere where it concerned his children when he had asked her to become their stepmother. She shook her head as if to rid it of the words they had hurtled at each other.

A day before Livia and Allison's grandparents drove to pick up their grandchildren to take them back to Florida for spring break. That was before she planned to spend three days with her parents before returning to The Falls to spend some alone time with Aiden.

Spring had come to the South and as she drove, she noticed it was slowly making its way northward. She maneuvered into the driveway to the home where she'd grown up and smiled when she saw the pussy willow bush she'd planted decades before. The front door opened and Taryn waved through the windshield at her mother when she stepped onto the front porch.

She knew what she would look like at fifty-eight because she was a younger version of her mother. Mildred was off the porch as soon as Taryn got out of the Pathfinder. She kissed Mildred's cheek. "Hi, gorgeous."

Mildred hugged Taryn. "I must admit, you're looking good yourself." She held her at arm's length. "You even put on a little weight."

Taryn reached for her mother's hand. "That's because I'm relaxed and eating three meals a day."

"Come inside and rest yourself. Your grandmother went to visit a friend who hasn't been feeling well, while Father is off golfing with some of his buddies."

"Mom, I don't believe it. You put in for vacation so we all could be together and Dad's off golfing."

Mildred led Taryn through the living and dining rooms and into the large ultramodern kitchen. "We'd planned to do things together before Langdon called to say his country needs him."

"Is Julie coming with the boys?"

"No. She decided to take the kids to Miami because her sister has been pestering her to come and live in Florida."

Taryn refrained from telling her mother that Langdon did not like his sister-in-law and there was no way he was going to move his family from Virginia Beach to Miami. "So, there's just you and me."

Mildred smiled. "So it seems. Did you stop to eat?"

"No. I wanted to drive straight through. I'm going to wash my hands and then raid the fridge."

"Don't bother. I'll fix you a plate. We had leftover chicken, so I made salad. I also have some deviled eggs and potato salad."

"It all sounds good," Taryn said as she walked to the half bath off the kitchen.

"After you eat, you have to tell me about the family you're living with."

"Okay." Taryn had sent her mother photos of Aiden, Livia and Allison. She returned to the kitchen to find a salad plate, along with a tall glass of iced tea. She loved her mother's cooking, and as soon as she was old enough to look over the stove, she had become Mildred's sous chef.

"How is it living with a single father and his children?"

Mildred's question opened the door for Taryn to tell her mother everything—including Aiden's marriage proposal.

"Have you said yes?"

"No, Mom."

"Why not?"

"I just don't feel the need to rush into anything." Suddenly the floodgates opened and she told her mother about her disagreement with Aiden. "I can't marry a man who wants me as his wife, but draws the line when it comes to his children."

"Perhaps he was upset seeing his ex-wife again," Mildred said softly. "It probably brought back horrific memories for him."

"Why are you taking his side, Mom?"

"I'm not taking his side, Taryn. You need to see both sides. It's obvious Aiden loves you, otherwise he never would've asked you to marry him. And you've told me how much he appreciates what you've done with his daughters. I'm certain he'll be sorry he said what he did once he thinks about it."

A hint of a smile flittered over Taryn's mouth. "Spoken like a true social worker."

"I'm not talking to you like a social worker, but your mother. You've had enough unhappiness in your life, so you're past due for a happy ever after."

Taryn's smile widened. "Why do I feel as if I'm a heroine in a romance novel?"

"Maybe it's because you are." Mildred ran a hand over her short stylishly coiffed salt-and-pepper hair. "I wasn't going to say anything, but James stopped by a couple of months ago looking for you."

Taryn froze, the fork poised in midair. "What did he want?"

"He said he wanted to apologize for hurting you and would like another chance."

She shook her head. "That will never happen."

"I told him you'd moved down South and you were living with a single father and his daughters."

"Well, that is the truth."

"He said as long as you're not married, he feels he has a chance to make it right again."

"Mom, please! Single, married or divorced, I don't want anything to do with James Robinson. He had his chance and he blew it. What I don't understand is his driving all the way out here when he could've called or sent me a text because I didn't change my number. And maybe I should send him a text and tell him to stay the hell away from my family."

Mildred grimaced. "I knew I shouldn't have said anything because I've upset you."

"I'm not upset with you, Mom. I'm angry with James for having the audacity to come here acting as if all he has to do is be contrite and all will be forgiven. It's not going to happen and never will happen."

Mildred waved a hand as if sweeping away something. "Enough about James. Back to Aiden. Are you in love with him?" Taryn nodded. "Should I assume he's in love with you?" She nodded again. "What about his kids?"

"What about them?"

"Do you think they're putting pressure on their father to marry you because they want a mother like other children?"

Taryn was slightly taken aback by her mother's query. "Why all of the questions? I love Aiden and I love his children. And when I feel the time is right, I'll let him know whether I will or will not marry him." She wanted to tell her mother that given what Aiden had said to her earlier that morning she would not marry him. And Taryn didn't want to remind her mother that she still was legally bound to teach Aiden's children, with an option to renew for another year. "I'm going to take a nap because I got up before dawn to be on the road to beat the DC–Baltimore rush-hour traffic."

"Go and get some rest. We'll talk again when you get up."

As promised, Taryn returned to Wickham Falls three days later and when she maneuvered into the driveway, it was the first time she felt as if she had truly come home. She alighted from the SUV and walked up the porch and then she saw Aiden. A short beard covered his face and judging from the dark circles under his eyes it was apparent he hadn't had much sleep.

Aiden caught her arm when she attempted to brush past him. "Denise is an addict."

Taryn's body stiffened in shock. "How do you know?"

Aiden closed his eyes and when he opened them, they were filled with pain. "She tried to hide the tracks on her arms, but I saw them. There's no way I'm going to subject my daughters to seeing their mother strung out on drugs. They've had nothing but bad memories of Denise and I'd give up my life to keep them from going through that again. There were times when I wanted to shake her whenever she taunted me, saying she'd slept with other men to get enough money to leave Wickham Falls because she hated this town as much as the townsfolks hated her."

"Did you really believe her when she said she'd slept with other men?" Taryn asked.

"No. I think she said it to punish me.

"I'm sorry for transferring my rage from Denise onto you because you're the best thing to come into my life since becoming a father. I love you more than I've ever loved any woman, and if you don't mind spending the rest of your life with a gruff old man with a body that has been to hell and back, then I'm offering you my love, protection and hopefully the chance for you to make me a better man."

Taryn didn't see Aiden's tears because of the ones flooding her own eyes. Cradling his face in her hands, she felt the moisture on his cheeks. "I love you so much." She kissed every inch of his face and then his mouth. "And because I do, I'm going to marry you and become the mother of our children."

Aiden picked her up and spun her around. "When?"

"Next year."

He set her on her feet. "When next year?"

"October. I've always wanted an autumn wedding."

"But that's more than a year and a half away."

"Am I worth the wait, Aiden?"

He smiled and nodded his head. "Hell yeah!"

She reached for his hands. "Go back to work. I'll be here when you come back."

"You promise?"

"Yes. And you know I always keep my promises."

Taryn stood on the porch watching Aiden as he got back into his SUV and drove away. She'd gotten to see another side of her Wickham Falls SEAL's personality, and it was something she didn't want to witness ever again.

She hadn't told Aiden that her life had been fast-tracked the very day she moved into his house and setting a wedding date seventeen months away would allow her to slow down and plan her future with him and their children.

Seventeen months later, Taryn rested her hand on the sleeve of her father's tuxedo jacket as he led her down the carpet in the church where she, Aiden and their children attended services. The entire church was decorated with fall flowers in keeping with the season. Jessica was her matron of honor, Allison and Livia were flower girls, while Aiden had selected Lucas to be his best man. The church was filled with family, friends and past and present buddies from Aiden's SEAL team in their navy dress blues.

Aiden had opted for his dress blue uniform once the responses came in from his military buddies. It had taken her more than a month to select a gown and when she saw a strapless sheath dress with a chapel train she felt as if it had been designed for her. She'd pinned baby's breath in her upswept hairdo in lieu of a veil. The bouquet of fall flowers was held together with flowing yellow, red and orange ribbons.

She gave her mother and grandmother a sidelong glance when she passed their pew, noticing that both women were dabbing their eyes. Her gaze lingered on her brother in his own crisp blue uniform. It was obvious that the military was definitely represented.

Aiden reached for her hand before the minister asked who gave this woman in marriage, eliciting snickers from those in attendance. The diamonds in her rose gold engagement ring caught the overhead light. She was surprised when Aiden chose to wear a matching band in brushed rose gold.

He raised her right hand and kissed it before turning to face the minister. "I'm ready now," he said, his voice carrying easily throughout the church.

"Are you certain you're ready?" the minister, who served in the military as a chaplain, asked.

"Aye, aye, sir."

The entire church exploded in laughter as Taryn nudged her soon-to-be husband's foot. They managed to get through the ceremony and then the minister told Aiden he could kiss his wife.

Taryn pressed her mouth to his ear. "I'm six weeks' pregnant, and I hope it's a boy," she whispered.

Throwing back his head, he shouted, "Hooyah!"

The navy's shout-out echoed throughout the church and at the same time, a photographer captured the love in the newlyweds' eyes as they smiled at each other.

* * * * *

Look out for the next book in the
WICKHAM FALLS WEDDINGS *series,*
coming in September 2018!

And to make the wait feel shorter, check out these other great books by Rochelle Alers:

HOME TO WICKHAM FALLS
CLAIMING THE CAPTAIN'S BABY

Available now wherever Harlequin Special Edition books and ebooks are sold!

#2623 FORTUNE'S HOMECOMING
The Fortunes of Texas: The Rulebreakers • by Allison Leigh

Celebrity rodeo rider Grayson Fortune is seeking a reprieve from the limelight. So as his sweet real estate agent, Billie Pemberton, searches to find him the perfect home, he struggles to keep his mind on business. Grayson is sure he's not cut out for commitment, but Billie is convinced that love and family are Grayson's true birthright...

#2624 HER SEVEN-DAY FIANCÉ
Match Made in Haven • by Brenda Harlen

Confirmed bachelor Jason Channing has no intention of putting a ring on any woman's finger—until Alyssa Cabrera, his too-sexy neighbor, asks him a favor. But their engagement is just for a week...isn't it?

#2625 THE MAVERICK'S BRIDAL BARGAIN
Montana Mavericks • by Christy Jeffries

Cole Dalton thought letting Vivienne Shuster plan his wedding—to no one— would work out just fine for both of them. But now not only are they getting caught up in a lot of lies, they might just be getting caught up in each other!

#2626 COMING HOME TO CRIMSON
Crimson, Colorado • by Michelle Major

Escaping from a cheating fiancé in a "borrowed" car, Sienna Pierce can't think of anywhere to go but Crimson, the hometown she swore she'd never return to. When Sheriff Cole Bennet crosses her path, however, Crimson starts to look a little bit more like home.

#2627 MARRY ME, MAJOR
American Heroes • by Merline Lovelace

Alex needs a husband—fast! Luckily, he doesn't actually need to be around, so Air Force Major Benjamin Kincaid will do perfectly. That is, until he's injured—suddenly this marriage of convenience becomes much more than just a piece of paper...

#2628 THE BALLERINA'S SECRET
Wilde Hearts • by Teri Wilson

With her dream role in her grasp, Tessa needs to focus. But rehearsing with brooding Julian is making that very difficult. Will she be able to reveal the insecurities beneath her dancer's poise, or will her secret keep them apart?

HSECNM0518

Get 4 FREE REWARDS!

We'll send you 2 FREE Books plus 2 FREE Mystery Gifts.

Harlequin® Special Edition books feature heroines finding the balance between their work life and personal life on the way to finding true love.

FREE
Value Over
$20

*Cole Dalton thought letting Vivienne Shuster
plan his wedding—to no one—would work out just
fine for both of them. But now not only are they getting
caught up in a lot of lies, they might just be getting
caught up in each other!*

*Read on for a sneak preview of
the next MONTANA MAVERICKS story,
THE MAVERICK'S BRIDAL BARGAIN
by Christy Jeffries.*

"You're engaged?"

"Of course I'm not engaged." Cole visibly shuddered. "I'm not even boyfriend material, let alone husband material."

Confusion quickly replaced her anger and Vivienne could only stutter, "Wh-why?"

"I guess because I have more important things going on in my life right now than to cozy up to some female I'm not interested in and pretend like I give a damn about all this commitment crap."

"No, I mean why would you need to plan a wedding if you're not getting married?"

"You said you need to book another client." He rocked onto the heels of his boots. "Well, I'm your next client."

Vivienne shook her head as if she could jiggle all the scattered pieces of this puzzle into place. "A client who has no intention of getting married?"

"Yes. But it's not like your boss would know the difference."

"She might figure it out when no actual marriage takes place. If you're not boyfriend material, then does that mean you don't have a girlfriend? I mean, who would we say you're marrying?"

Okay, so that first question Vivienne threw in for her own clarification. Even though they hadn't exactly kissed, she needed reassurance that she wasn't lusting over some guy who was off-limits.

"Nope, no need for a girlfriend," he said, and she felt some of her apprehension drain. But then he took a couple of steps closer. "We can make something up, but why would it even need to get that far? Look, you just need to buy yourself some time to bring in more business. So you sign me up or whatever you need to do to get your boss off your back, and then after you bring in some more customers—legitimate ones—my fake fiancée will have cold feet and we'll call it off."

If her eyes squinted any more, they'd be squeezed shut. And then she'd miss his normal teasing smirk telling her that he was only kidding. But his jaw was locked into place and the set of his straight mouth looked dead serious.

Don't miss
THE MAVERICK'S BRIDAL BARGAIN
by Christy Jeffries,
available June 2018 wherever
Harlequin® Special Edition books and ebooks are sold.

www.Harlequin.com

The Rancher's
Secret Child
Brenda Minton

Save $1.00

on the purchase of any
Love Inspired® or
Love Inspired® Suspense book.

Available wherever books are sold,
including most bookstores, supermarkets,
drugstores and discount stores.

Save $1.00

on the purchase of any Love Inspired® or Love Inspired® Suspense book.

Coupon valid until July 30, 2018. Redeemable at participating retail outlets in the
U.S. and Canada only. Limit one coupon per customer.

52615678

5 65373 00076 2 (8100)0 12357

® and ™ are trademarks owned and used by the trademark owner and/or its licensee.

© 2018 Harlequin Enterprises Limited

LICOUP0518

USA TODAY bestselling author

SHEILA ROBERTS

returns with a brand-new series set on the charming Washington coast.

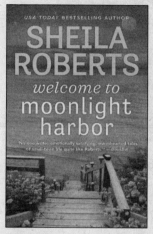

Once happily married, Jenna Jones is about to turn forty, and this year for her birthday—lucky her—she's getting a divorce. She's barely able to support herself and her teenage daughter, but now her deadbeat artist ex is hitting her up for spousal support...and then spending it on his "other" woman. Still, as her mother always says, every storm brings a rainbow. Then, she gets a very unexpected gift from her great-aunt. Aging Aunt Edie is finding it difficult to keep up her business running The Driftwood Inn, so she

invites Jenna to come and run the place. The town is a little more run-down than Jenna remembers, but that's nothing compared to the ramshackle state of The Driftwood Inn. But who knows? With the help of her new friends and a couple of handsome citizens, perhaps that rainbow is on the horizon after all.

Available now, wherever books are sold!

Looking for more satisfying love stories
with community and family at their core?

Check out **Harlequin® Special Edition**
and **Harlequin® Western Romance** books!

New books available every month!

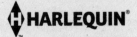